Mosaic of Seduction

The Possession Chronicles #1.5

By

Carrie Dalby

WINTER

Chapter One

Walking into the sea of darkness felt like coming home. Eliza Melling straightened the white mantilla on her head and took in the simple surroundings of The Church of the Assumption. The pine walls were pale in comparison to the olive skin and black clothing of the Italian parishioners—so different from the kaleidoscope of colors amid the stained glass of the cathedral in Mobile. Alexander huffed in annoyance when she gripped his arm, his free hand wiping his bloodshot eyes.

Two young deacons stood near the apse, but Eliza knew which one was Alexander's new friend by his chiseled features and broad shoulders. He would deny it, but her brother's fine taste extended from lovely women to the handsomest companions—not to mention expensive drinks and clothing. While Alexander knew which textures he enjoyed, Eliza had to teach him to dress in appropriate tones for his fair complexion, otherwise he looked washed out compared to his striking Mystics of Dardenne brothers. But even the combination of Easton, Woodslow, and Spunner fell short in comparison to the taller of the two deacons.

Alexander brought Eliza to a rear bench. She straightened his azure cravat before taking a seat. The deacon sported a dimpled grin though he walked with reverence in the church. Hand outstretched before he reached them, his gaze swept between the siblings.

"It is glorious to see you, Alexander." His velvety voice strummed Eliza's soul as he kissed her brother's cheeks in greeting. "I am glad you made the effort to attend Mass. May I have an introduction to your ..."

"Sister," Alexander said. "Claudio, this is Eliza. She followed me across the bay to Seacliff Cottage yesterday morning. Eliza, Deacon Claudio De Fiore."

She offered her hand and Claudio stepped forward to kiss her cheeks when he took it. Her finger brushed the coarse fabric of his cassock's sleeve as she breathed in his scent before he stepped back. Basil and sage—earthy and delicious.

"It appears we share the same concern over my brother, Deacon De Fiore. Please tell me you're joining us for dinner and will help me talk sense into Alex. He's behaved abominably this week and kept a bottle with him yesterday when he wasn't riding."

A slight frown graced Claudio's lips before he nodded. "*Sí*, I am permitted to visit your home after Mass. I shall need to return to the rectory by five this afternoon, but I am at your disposal until then."

"That's wonderful to hear, isn't it, Alex?" Eliza fingered the mantilla over her hair and smiled at the deacon before looking to her brother. "We could even ride back to Daphne with the deacon and catch the evening ferry here."

"That's a splendid idea," Alexander said. "We'll see you out front afterward, Claudio." He waited until the deacon walked the nave before dropping on the pew beside Eliza. "You're shameless for flirting with a deacon and wearing a white mantilla."

"I can't change to black and you know it," she whispered. "Father would kill me."

"Then at least be honest with yourself and switch to a hat."

"Like Lucy?" She regretted the words as soon as Alexander's fist clenched. She grasped his hand in her own. "She still loves you, Alex. The same as you feel for her. Lucy tried to do right before God so you two could progress. I have no reason to seek forgiveness in an attempt to set my life right. Maybe if I experience love, I'll be driven to seek penance for my actions."

"You mustn't live your life as I have mine, Eliza." His words were drowned by the organ notes booming through the humble space.

***

Claudio sat beside Alexander in the fine carriage, doing his best not to stare at Eliza's blue-violet eyes. Sitting across from the young woman, he could not help but study the most amazing hue he had ever encountered in his twenty-four years. Behind the vivid color was an aching darkness that almost matched her brother's in its pain. Remembering his own sister's eyes as she lay on her deathbed two years previous, Claudio wished to heal as he could not accomplish in those final hours, no matter how hard he had prayed.

But this day he was there for the elder Melling sibling. Red-rimmed eyes betrayed Alexander's day of alcohol as loudly as his sister had proclaimed it the previous hour.

"Mass was wonderful, no?" Claudio said to him. "Were you able to feel the spirit though you could not understand the words?"

Alexander ran a hand through his hair, rumpling it so it matched his countenance. "I feel nothing these days."

"I felt the powers of Heaven battling the Hell within." Eliza leaned forward, placing a hand on Claudio's knee. "I've never been to a more stimulating Mass. Americans need more of the passion Italians bring to everything."

Claudio grinned before seeing the cutting look Alexander gave his sister. She sat back on her bench but did not lose eye contact with the deacon. The warm spot where her gloved hand had rested on his leg burned as much as her inviting gaze. He crossed himself. *Padre, perdonami.*

When they came to a stop before Seacliff Cottage, Claudio hesitantly lifted his eyes to the gothic arches of the windows—all the way to the third floor of the white house.

"The house is most extraordinary," he remarked as they stepped onto the massive porch.

Alexander brushed past Claudio, opened the front door then stepped to the side. His sister breezed through the doorway, then Alexander motioned to the deacon.

Moving forward, Claudio's body stiffened in the entry. *Non entrare!* The warning of "do not enter" was loud in his mind, his soul disturbed by an unknown presence. He turned to his host. The pain in Alexander's pale eyes solidified the deacon's purpose.

I shall not leave a soul in need. Claudio crossed himself and strode over the tainted threshold with one hand on his crucifix.

In the front hall, Eliza removed her gloves and capelet. Alexander kicked away his shoes, removed his tie, and peeled off his suit jacket.

"Your cassock, Deacon De Fiore?" Eliza held a delicate hand toward him to accept his frock.

Their mutual gaze tugged him closer to her alluring presence. He fingered her bare hand before raising it to his lips then shaking his head. "Not today, *signorina.*"

A challenge flashed in her eyes. "Then one day soon." She took his arm and led him into the parlor.

Alexander was already seated beside a decanter trio, a half-empty glass in hand. Waving it, he nodded to the table. "What will you have?"

"Bourbon!" Eliza declared. "For both of us."

Seeing Claudio's hesitation, Alexander stood. "No, Eliza. The deacon will have wine or sherry."

"Then red wine," she replied as she went for goblets. "We'll pretend we're partaking of sacramental emblems and confess our misdeeds."

Alexander slung back the remainder of his glass and discarded it on the credenza. "There aren't enough hours in the day for me to bare all mine, but let's gather in the dining room." Snatching the brandy and a bottle of wine, he stalked down the dark hall.

"I've never seen him this bad," Eliza whispered when she took Claudio's proffered arm. He relieved her of the wine glasses and they joined Alexander at the massive table. "Prepare the drinks and I'll collect the food, Alex."

When Eliza was gone, Alexander took several swigs directly from his bottle.

"This can be of no help," Claudio told him. "You need to fortify yourself in preparation for tomorrow. You will work, no?"

"Yes, and I have a court date Tuesday morning."

"And you have settled in your mind that you will not return to the corrupt house you frequented last week?"

Alexander shrugged.

"If you wish to win Lucy back, you must put in the effort to cleanse your life."

Eliza glided into the room with a large serving tray. "Preach to him, Deacon De Fiore. My errant brother needs his queen back in his life. There were never two souls suited for each other as Alex and Lucy."

"If you cared so much for my standing with Lucy, you never should have thrown yourself at her brother!"

Her pale cheeks pinked and she bit her lip as she lowered her head. "I told you I was sorry about that. I'll do my part to help secure restitution."

"Forget it and leave me to my misery, Eliza Rose." He sunk back into his chair, bringing the bottle to his lips once more.

Hoping to change the subject, Claudio latched onto the new information. Turning to Eliza, he smiled reassuringly. "We both have botanical names. *Fiore* means flower."

Her vibrant smile returned. "Then we'll be sure to grow together."

Chapter Two

As soon as Eliza and Alexander exited the ferry, she spotted their mother's chauffeur beyond the dock. "Did you request the automobile?"

"No. Did you tell her where you were going when you left yesterday?"

"Not exactly, but I hinted at it over supper Friday."

"Then you must be in trouble. I hope it was worth it."

Eliza smiled. "Anything is worth it to have met Claudio De Fiore."

"Master Melling, Miss Melling." The driver opened the rear door and took their luggage. "Your mother sent me for you."

"Thank you." Eliza slid into the back of the limousine, Alexander following her.

They didn't speak on the way home, and as soon as they were in the marble foyer, Alexander cut for the stairs.

"Alexander Randolph and Eliza Rose," their mother's voice called from the gilded parlor. "Come here at once."

The siblings shuffled in, elbowing each other like they'd done as children, trying to get the other to take the lead.

"Really, Alexander! You've been gone weeks and then reappear behaving as a child." Ruth Melling's eyes stabbed from her son to her daughter. "And you, Eliza, should know better than to run off alone during your debut season. I'll not have a scandal about you ruining your prospects. Our family has been the topic of enough gossip the past two months thanks to that brazen blonde who had her eyes on our fortune."

Alexander gripped the back of the nearest chair, and Eliza stepped forward.

"Lucy never wanted our money, Mother. She and Alex are deeply in love."

"Then why did she run from him after he broke ties with his father?" Ruth sniffed and raised her chin. "If she had truly loved him, she would have stayed, inheritance or not. Alex is charming and—"

"She ran because I showed her who I really am—another merciless Melling wishing to rule over everyone around him!" Alexander stomped up the stairs and slammed his bedroom door.

Ruth sighed and looked to her daughter. "You came to no harm on your journey across the bay?"

"No, Mother."

"Turn around."

Eliza did so.

Her mother sighed once more. "You look positively bloated. Only soup for the next two days. You must look your best for the Mystic Order of Sirens masquerade Tuesday evening. Now go wash up. I'll send the maid to your room with a cup of broth for your supper."

***

"Mother, please!" Eliza screeched as Ruth pulled the laces on her corset. "I won't be able to move."

"If you stopped eating all those sweets, this would not be such an ordeal." She yanked the cords again.

"I'll spew all over the floor if you tighten me another millimeter!"

"Really, Eliza." She turned her daughter about, spanning her fingers around her waist. "That is the best I can do with you today. You will need to diet for a week before the next engagement."

Eliza stood in the middle of her room after her mother left the door open after her exit. Moments later, George Melling took in the sight of his daughter in her underclothes and corset with the eye of a man appraising livestock.

"You'll wear the new blue gown tonight?" he asked.

"Yes, sir." Eliza lifted her head, determined not to be cowed by his cold stare.

"Looking as you do and blessed with my family's name, you're sure to secure plenty of invitations. The more mystic societies you have ties with, the better your chances will be with your art. Portraits are well sought after."

"I have no ambition to paint debutantes, Father. There's only one who interests me artistically, and I was already lucky enough to sketch her."

George smirked. "I know Alex spoke of having Lucille's portrait made, but their engagement didn't last long enough for that. Such a pity. She is indeed lovely to look upon."

"If you had left Alex alone rather than—"

He raised his arm to backhand her cheek, but paused above her menacingly. "It's no concern of yours, Eliza. Remember that. I'll let my hand fall sometime when there's no party to attend. Don't forget that you owe me for all I've done for you."

She bit the inside of her lip to keep it from trembling.

"Keep looking as you do and I'll find you a husband worthy of a Melling." He patted her cheek before leaving.

Frozen in anger and entrapped in her confining shapewear, Eliza could do no more than cry within her prison.

"Don't let them get to you, Eliza Rose." Alexander came in and closed the door behind him, holding a small box of chocolates like an offering.

A sob caught in her throat, and she clutched her aching sides.

"God knows you have it worse than me in many ways," he said. "Allow me to help." He tossed the gift on the end of the bed and reached for her laces. The knot their mother had tied was no match for his nimble fingers.

Eliza breathed freely and turned to him once the corset was tied in a more realistic fashion. "Thank you, Alex. You're remarkably skilled with corsets. Do I want to know how many women you've unlaced?"

His impish smile flashed before darkness caught his memories. "Only one that matters, though there was plenty of practice before her."

"And after." She held his icy gaze. "You didn't come home last night. Not to mention last week's debauchery."

"I cleared my personal things from the duplex and won't be going back." He ran a hand through his blond hair. "I needed relief after seeing to that yesterday evening."

"You'll not find relief where you pay for the experience, though I'm sure those girls heap you with praise and pleasantries. You're not the type that needs their services like sour-faced Rupert."

Eliza opened the box and bit into a chocolate. "These are doubly delicious after two days of soup. Thank you."

He nodded and turned away.

"Are you attending the masquerade?"

Alexander shook his head and opened the door.

"You could escort me."

"I'm not in the mood, but enjoy it, Eliza." He returned to kiss her cheek. "And for the love of God, behave yourself."

"And you, Alexander. Don't go to the district tonight."

"I'm locking myself in my room."

After he left, Eliza pulled on her heeled slippers and stepped into her blue gown. By the time her mother returned, all that needed to be done were the final buttons on the back of her dress and tying on her coordinating black-and-blue satin mask.

Her father waited at the bottom of the stairs, watching Judith McGowan bedecked in red with a hungry leer.

"You look divine, Eliza!" Judith exclaimed. "Thank you, Mr. and Mrs. Melling, for allowing your daughter to accompany me." She tucked an arm through Eliza's, the other hand going to her hip as she angled toward George. "You have the prettiest debutante of the season."

His posture straightened, though Eliza didn't know whether it was from the compliment to his daughter or the view of the shapeliest form in Mobile. "We trust you to chaperone well, Miss McGowan."

Once the two young women were in the carriage, Judith dug in for the latest news. "I suppose your brother won't make an appearance tonight. I heard he was seen stumbling to work several days last week from the direction of the district. If I hadn't already heard stories about his escapades there, I might've assumed that wallflower Lucy Easton had taught him to appreciate a new level of passion."

"He's stayed drunk since the separation, but the district has no bearing on their falling out," Eliza said.

Judith laughed. "Not according to my sources. Word is the Dardennes were celebrating Edmund's engagement and no fewer than a dozen whores were seen spilling out of your brother's house in the middle of the night along with the men."

Eliza waved her hand in dismissal, happy that her own name hadn't been mentioned. "You know how men are during Carnival.

I'm sure the reports were grossly exaggerated. Alex is no worse this year than he's been during any other Mardi Gras. In fact, he's improved. Lucy did manage to subdue him."

"Obviously not enough. I've said it before but I'll say it again—he's going to have to find a bride from out of town when he wishes to marry, because no one here will put up with his history. Let's hope the men won't mind him being your brother when they're seeking a wife, although your mother is beyond reproach. I'm sure the gentlemen's own mothers will put in a good word for your pure character as her daughter."

Eliza smiled demurely. "Yes, let's hope."

Temperance Hall, the site of the Mystics of Dardenne ball Eliza had attended just over a month ago, was the location of the respectable Mystic Order of Sirens masquerade hosted by a group of young ladies who had banded together two years previous. They were one of the only societies that didn't wear costumes to their own ball. Instead, they dressed to subtly blend in with the decorations. The bold crimson of Judith's gown was striking beside Eliza's royal blue as they entered the star-spangled-themed party. Many of the other women were in white and gold, and all eyes fell to the newcomers. Giddy with the attention, Eliza suffered through a greeting from Kate Stuart who then set upon Judith.

Free from her chaperone, Eliza took a glass of champagne and traveled the room in search of an enticing form. Even with embellished masks, the men were shapeless nothings compared to the vision of Deacon De Fiore that she'd kept in her mind the past two days.

"Miss Melling." A firm hand took her elbow. "I'm surprised to see you tonight."

She turned to the chip-toothed smile of Sean Spunner. "How good of you to still speak with me."

"I won't let your brother's folly stop me from dancing with you." His grin doubled as he offered his hand. "Would you share the next with me, Miss Melling?"

"Only if you call me Eliza."

The orchestra paused between the songs.

"All right, Eliza." He took her into position for a waltz and tugged her close to whisper in her ear. "As long as you don't expect me to moan your name like Eddie Easton did."

She laughed. "You don't think less of me because of that night?"

"I like your spunk," he said as he led her in a dignified sway. "You're bold like your brother, and he's always fun to be around. If Mystics of Dardenne accepted females, I'd initiate you in a heartbeat."

Pressing so that there was no space between them, she studied the gap the chip made in his teeth, wondering how it would feel to run her tongue along it. "How would you initiate me? Would it involve the typical shenanigans?"

"Nothing typical for you, Eliza," he whispered before licking the shell of her ear.

She giggled and pressed against him once more before dropping back into a respectable stance. "Alex was right."

Sean tilted his head, cheeky smile gracing his face. "About what?"

"He told me months ago to drop my pursuit of Edmund and go for you instead. He said you'd romance me and that Eddie was boring when it came to women."

"The Easton charm doesn't translate well to intimacies?"

She laughed and shook her head. "I think *I* taught him a thing or two instead of the other way around."

"Are you ready to try out a real Dardenne?" His hand on her hip migrated toward her backside. "I saw you arrive with Judith, but she'll be too wrapped up in trying to catch a millionaire to notice if you slip away with me."

"I appreciate the offer, Sean, but I do need to see Edmund. Do you expect him tonight? I want to ask after Lucy."

"He arrived with Mary Margaret, but I don't think he'd allow a moment with you. She found out about his bachelor party, and he's playing the part of doting fiancé for now."

"We'll see about that."

"I'll bet you a dollar he won't say a word to you."

"And I'll raise you a fiver he takes me aside or dances with me."

"You were the best poker player that night. It's a deal." The song came to a close, and they shook hands to seal the bet. "I'll be watching."

Eliza scanned the room over the rim of her fresh wine glass. Edmund stood in a grouping with Dr. John Woodslow, Mary Margaret, and another young lady with eyes set too far apart that Eliza vaguely recognized from the parish.

"Hello, everyone." Eliza smiled, gaze roaming between the men. "It's a lovely masquerade, isn't it? I adore the stars hanging from the ceiling. And it goes well with your gold gown, Mary Margaret. I feel rather like a stain on the party in my blue when so many of the ladies are in heavenly colors."

Mary Margaret and her friend purposely looked away from Eliza without comment. Edmund raised his glass and gazed at the hanging stars.

"Don't worry over costumes, Miss Melling," John said with his pronounced drawl. "Some ladies don't have the coloring to pull off bold schemes like you can. You're a striking sight."

Grateful for the doctor's kindness, she flashed him her winning smile and was rewarded with a wink. He was another poker-playing Dardenne who knew how audacious she was.

"You're very kind, Dr. Woodslow." She stepped closer to the others, a hand reaching for Edmund's arm. "I was hoping for a word with Mr. East—"

Mary Margaret slapped Eliza's hand away. "You have no right to approach Edmund after what your brother did to his sister!"

Mouth open in surprise, Eliza sputtered. "It's none of my doing what hap—"

"My parents almost made me call off the wedding!" Mary Margaret snapped. "Especially when they heard that Alexander hosted a drunken party with women of the evening and forced poor Edmund into it."

Eliza laughed so hard that she snorted. Regaining her composure, she patted Edmund's shoulder. "Bless your heart. That party must have been a shock to you."

Edmund turned scarlet, and John covered a laugh with a cough. "Would you honor me with a dance, Miss Melling?"

"Gladly, Dr. Woodslow." When they turned toward the dancefloor, Eliza caught sight of Sean and motioned in his direction. "Could we stop by your friend first?"

"Of course."

"I'll not doubt you again, Sean." Eliza pulled a five dollar bill from her reticule and kissed his cheek as she handed it over. "Well played."

"Any time, Eliza." He pocketed the money and slapped his society brother on the back. "Don't keep her too long. I want another dance with her."

Eliza was all giggles as she and John twirled around the room, but her smile faded when they waltzed past Judith with a broad-shouldered man who filled out his tuxedo better than any man in the room—Frederick Davenport. She hadn't expected to see him there and would have thought he'd be comforting Lucy.

"Dr. Woodslow, would you be a dear and cut in on Frederick for me? I'd like to talk to him, but I don't know when a double rush will happen."

"Anything for a lady in need." John quickened their pace, bringing them alongside the other couple. "Excuse me, Davenport."

Not waiting for an answer, John danced off with Judith, leaving Eliza standing awkwardly before the imposing stature of Frederick in a white mask.

"Frederick, I—"

"Good evening, Miss Melling." He took hold of her with a fluid grace that made her ache to see him in the boxing ring. "You look well tonight."

"Are you here with Lucy?" she blurted.

His lips pressed together and he shook his head. "She hasn't left the house since I brought her home last Saturday."

"Is she unwell?"

"Heartsick, but she types that manuscript for the publisher all day."

Eliza frowned. "Does she allow you to comfort her?"

"I sit with her in the evenings after supper. I told her of this ball, letting her know I would decline if she needed me. She insisted that I come. I think she wished me to see if Alexander was here."

"He's locked himself in his room tonight. He's pained, Frederick. He loves her and feels terrib—"

"He deserves his pain." Frederick's hand nearly crushed Eliza's in his grasp. "I've heard how he spent last week, as though Lucy was nothing but another woman to bed in his unending conquests."

"Father taught him to—"

"Your father is despicable, but Alexander is a fool for thinking he can keep blaming his father for his mistakes. He needs to act like a man and not a victim if he's to make anything of himself. I pray he suffers long, because I know Lucy will be scarred for life over this."

Eliza stepped out of Frederick's embrace, staring at the hatred burning in his brown eyes that all the ladies in town claimed were the kindest on Earth.

"He loves her," she whispered. "Please let Lucy know how sorry he is and that he wants another ch—"

"He's already had another chance," Frederick said through gritted teeth. "If I have anything to say about it, that Melling scum will never come close enough to utter another word to Lucy. He's done enough damage."

"You think she's yours now, do you?" Eliza countered. "You think you've won her hand because you stood by while she and my brother had a misunderstanding?"

"No one could mistake what his unholy intentions were when he chased her through the duplex, yelling about having her however he wanted."

"That's *passion*, Mr. Davenport." Eliza held her ground on the edge of the dancefloor. "You might eventually win Lucy's hand, but you'll never gain her passion. That's something a woman can only give to one man in her lifetime, and it will always belong to Alexander."

Chapter Three

On the Sabbath before Lent, Claudio was seated and Mass about to begin when he saw Alexander and Eliza settling on the back pew. After the service, the deacon made his way to them while greeting parishioners.

"Alexander, it is good to see you looking well." Claudio kissed both his cheeks.

"He's stayed sober more often than not this past week," Eliza said.

Turning to her, Claudio greeted her in the same fashion—trying not to marvel over her creamy skin. "And you are *bellissimo*, Eliza."

Blue-violet eyes shining, she clung to his arm a moment. "I feel the light of God when I'm here."

Alexander took his sister's elbow and pulled her beside him. "Will you be able to visit us during the next few days, Claudio?"

"*Sí.* Tomorrow, if it is good for you."

"It's fine. When can you arrive?"

"Midday. I shall need to return by six."

They said their farewells then Claudio returned to Father Angelo for guidance on how to complete his duties after the final parishioners left. He spent his hours after dinner in contemplation, but still the vision of Eliza danced in his mind.

* * *

When he walked up the drive from the main road at noon on Monday, Claudio found Alexander grooming his horse in the yard.

"Good day, Alexander."

"Claudio, welcome. How skilled are you at riding?"

"I am not practiced in jumping, but I do ride."

"That's good enough." Alexander tossed an arm around his shoulders and kissed his cheeks first. "Your Italian ways are growing on me."

Laughing, Claudio thumped his back in a half-hug. "It helps me feel at home."

"Eliza!" Alexander yelled. "Saddle Flora with my old tack."

"It would be too heavy, no? I will help."

Claudio found Eliza in the second stall with a speckled mare. She radiated beauty in her hunter green riding habit. "Good day, *signorina.*"

She laid the blanket pad on her horse's back then flung her arms around Claudio. They kissed each other's cheeks, pausing to smile while still in contact.

"Alex looks better, doesn't he?" she whispered. "He only had three drinks after supper last night."

"*Sí,* his coloring is good."

"He loves to ride. We both do. We were gone hours yesterday afternoon." Eliza trailed her fingers down the buttons of Claudio's cassock. "You must remove this."

She stepped away with a teasing smile as she picked up the saddle. Claudio could not help but return the grin as he reached to take the saddle from her. He set it gently on Flora, and Eliza crouched to secure the buckle.

"Why does the coachman not ready your horse?" Claudio asked. "Or Alexander? It is too much for you to handle."

"Campbell is older than our father, and we enjoying seeing to our own horses when we're here. Besides, Deacon De Fiore, I'm stronger than I look. Never forget that."

Eliza secured the reins and led Flora out of the stable.

"Hang your vestment on one of the pegs, Claudio," Alexander said when he came to the doorway.

Eliza raised her eyebrows at Claudio and brought Flora's head down to whisper in the horse's ear. As soon as his cassock hung in the stable, he joined the siblings in the yard. Alexander tied a sack onto the back of Flora's saddle and swung into place on Janus.

"Come on, Eliza." He held a hand out to his sister.

With a smile that sent Claudio's heart soaring, she accepted Alexander's arm. Foot in the stirrup, she lifted her other leg to span the stallion as he pulled her up. The movement revealed her expertly camouflaged split skirt. She perched behind her brother, and Claudio grinned at the boldness of the young woman as he mounted her horse.

He followed Alexander's lead down a path to the bay, enjoying the view of Eliza more than he should. When the Mellings stopped in the sand, he brought Flora beside them. Eliza rested her cheek on her brother's back and watched Claudio with interest.

"Are you ready for some fun?" Alexander's tone was challenging.

"*Sí*. Tell me what to do."

"Keep up!" With a repeating yelp like a rabid animal, Alexander's heels touched Janus and they leapt southward.

Following their gallop, Claudio encouraged Flora to the same speed. They tore through the shallow river that fed into the bay and to the compacted sand beyond. The horse seemed well-versed in the race. Claudio kept a loose hold on the reins and allowed Flora to set the pace, which evened out once they closed the gap with Janus.

Eliza often looked back to check his progress, once even blowing him a kiss before her arms were back around Alexander. Under piers and passing the base of cliffs, the horses thundered on for miles. Well beyond the final scenes of humanity, Alexander slowed. Following the curve of the land, he turned left along an inlet into a quiet sanctuary.

Under the shade of a scraggly tree, Eliza dismounted.

"Welcome to Weeks Bay," she greeted Claudio when he stopped. Taking Flora's reins, she stroked her horse. "You brought him here safely, Flora. Thank you."

After Claudio dismounted, Eliza led the mare to a patch of cleared land near a freshwater stream and admonished the horse to stay nearby. She returned to the shade with the sack from the saddle.

"Our luncheon!" She raised the bag in triumph.

Alexander set Janus free as Eliza had done with her horse. He lit a cigarette and paced the shore as he smoked.

Claudio motioned to him, looking to Eliza. "Should I—"

She shook her head. "It's his way of coming down from the rush of the ride. He needs to transition to stillness since his own company isn't something he often likes to keep."

"Your insight into your brother's soul is remarkable. I am glad he has you."

"*He* isn't always glad, but we do get on more often than not. It's been a trying season for both of us. Between my debut, his whirlwind romance, and dealing with our parents, agony sums it up nicely."

Hoping to lift her mood, he sought her advice. "And how might I transition from the ride?" Claudio rubbed his upper legs through his black trousers. "I fear my body has grown soft with my church responsibilities."

"Never allow that to happen, Deacon De Fiore. Your lines are exquisite." Eliza's hands ran from his shoulders to biceps. Gazing up at him, her tongue traced the seam of her lips as her finger followed his jaw. "God formed you perfectly."

His body hummed with her touch. "There is beauty in all God's creations, and you are heavenly, Eliza." The tilt of her head was welcoming and he wanted nothing more than to feel her lips against his.

Alexander saved them with his return. "The picnic, Eliza, lest you forget why we're here."

She laughed in her confident way and settled on the sand. After opening the sack, she passed the wine to Alexander. "We'll have to share the bottle since I didn't pack glasses. Our communion by the sea. Claudio will break the bread for us."

He accepted the crusty loaf. "Then allow me to pray over it first."

Retrieving a handkerchief, he placed the bread on it. The three joined hands and Claudio prayed in Italian. Alexander and Eliza both said amen, and the food and wine passed freely between all.

Bread, cheese, fruit, and wine—the classic feast of lovers in the outdoors, and Claudio relished it. Since the Melling family had visited Italy five years past, they spoke of his country and the customs of the area. By the time the bottle was almost empty, Claudio's face was sore from smiling.

Eliza went to her knees beside her brother. "Tell him about Mardi Gras, Alex, and how people indulge before Lent to help them with their spiritual fast. You Dardenne brothers always do so well with the first half of the equation."

She settled beside him, her finger drawing shapes in the sand as Alexander unfolded the story of lavish parties, alcohol, stimulants, and sexual encounters that made Claudio blush.

"It sounds like an excuse to be immoral," the deacon said as he ate the final strawberry.

"Don't we all deserve an outlet?" Eliza asked as her finger trailed steadily closer to Claudio. She shifted onto her knees, right arm reaching forward as the squiggling line paused before his legs. "Surely the Lord will forgive us because he knows we're nothing but imperfect children."

He held her enchanting gaze. "Imperfect children who make mistakes are one thing, but those who willfully rebel and choose wickedness have a more difficult time finding forgiveness."

"Do you speak from experience?" Her lips curled in a delicious smile as she rested her hand on his knee.

"No more than the next man."

Alexander took the last swig of wine and fell back in the sand, limbs extended. "I've yet to find relief from my sins. Each new one buries me deeper in despair over the last."

"Surely confession will help," Eliza offered. "Confess to Claudio."

"I am not yet a priest. It would do him no good other than possibly making it easier to speak of it the next time."

"Then may I play the part of priest?" she said. "I'd like to hear the details of your transgressions."

Alexander kicked a leg toward her. "Go, Eliza Rose. Allow me to rest before we return to Seacliff." He rolled to his side, tucking an arm under his head and scrunching his legs toward his torso as though trying to leave as little of himself in the world as possible.

Eliza stood and reached for Claudio. Holding hands, she led him further around the inlet.

"Where are we going?" Claudio asked.

"The swamp. I want to show you an alligator."

"*Alligatore?* No, *signorina*, it is too dangerous!"

"They're just waking from their dormant months and are slow until the weather warms. Alexander and I do this every spring. There's a massive one I swear grows two feet each year. He'll surely be close to twenty feet in length this time."

They were on a footpath faded with dead branches and leaves from lack of use, making their way alongside a stagnant stream.

"Eliza, I am not comfortable with this plan. I do not wish to see you come to harm."

She paused at the top of a rise, a scant two feet drop to the creek from the bare earth. "You care for me, Claudio?"

"*Si,* and I do not wish to return to your brother and explain that an *alligatore* ate you for dinner."

"Oh, Claudio. Have *faith.*" She took his other hand in hers, squeezing them both to a pumping rhythm that mimicked his racing heart.

"I put my trust in God, not man."

"Or woman." Her eyebrows rose in challenge. "I trust you with my soul, Claudio. Won't you return the favor?"

"Will you come with me to Alexander?"

"Of course." Her arms snaked around his waist like a serpent in Eden. Her smile sought to lead him astray, and Claudio was ready for the beguilement. "You need to relax. It's Mardi Gras season. You heard all that Alex said. A token of affection would be nothing compared to a debauched masquerade."

"You are too beautiful, Eliza." He tucked a loose strand of hair behind her ear. "If you had found me on your travels through Italy, I would have run away with you."

She giggled and pressed closer. "I was a girl then, but I'm a woman now. Kiss me."

He started to shake his head, but one of her porcelain hands stroked his cheek.

"You will be a balm to my soul, Claudio. Heal me."

Her silken lips were not benign when he leaned in to gift a simple kiss. Her velvet tongue worked in tandem with a hand in his hair and the other at his waist, tugging him closer to her core as she moved against him. Eliza's pleasure pulled him into her enjoyment until it eclipsed his own.

"Eliza ..." He breathed her name as his mouth fell to her neck.

An instant later, she stepped out of his arms, looking demure. "That's all for today, Deacon De Fiore. It isn't Mardi Gras until tomorrow."

Afraid that shock would leave him immobile, he clutched his rosary as he took in the realization of his actions that had left his body stirred to a level he had not allowed since preparing for his *sacri ordines.*

Eliza brought his fist to her lips and kissed his rosary. "It was not sin, but bringing pleasure to another. I declare you the keeper of my soul, and that most certainly raised my spirit. Look there." She pointed to the tall grass on the other side of the low creek. "Do you see how the alligator watches us? Maybe he'll wish to mate now. After it feeds, of course."

A breeze rustled the reeds and the alligator snapped in reflex, giant mouth gnashing the air as his beast of a tail thrashed.

"My bite can be just as bad as his." Eliza hugged Claudio's arm and laughed. "Let's go tell Alex we saw him!"

They practically ran to the picnic spot—her youthful exuberance setting the pace.

Alexander wiped the sleep from his eyes as he listened to his sister's tale of the giant reptile, then they brought their horses over and both men mounted. Alexander leaned out for Eliza, but she swung onto Flora, heels striking the horse's flanks as soon as an arm was about Claudio.

"Eliza!" Alexander shouted. "It isn't proper!"

"But it is! All flowers must stay together in a garden of delight!" She nestled against Claudio's back, arms linked low about his waist.

He knew he could not deny the growing need to be with this rose of a woman who made him feel alive.

SPRING

Chapter Four

Eliza spent every other weekend at Seacliff Cottage with Alexander, who hosted Claudio for several hours on Saturday or Sunday afternoons. Never did she try to be familiar with the deacon other than in greeting or parting. She kept her distance to prevent overwhelming him, hoping he would remain as smitten with her while she quietly sketched him from across the room or picnic spot and gloried over his stature on Sunday mornings in church.

On the sixteenth of May, Eliza held her brother's arm as they ascended the steps to the Cathedral of the Immaculate Conception in downtown Mobile for the noon wedding Mass of Edmund Albert Easton and Mary Margaret Fitzgerald.

Circling a column like Folly in his approach, Sean's golden eyes sparked mischief. "Have you come to celebrate escaping Edmund's clutches?"

Laughing, Eliza offered her hand. "You know me well, Sean."

He kissed the back of her glove. "How about another wager? I say Edmund will grimace before saying his vows, maybe even taking on a greenish tint."

Alexander scowled. "Betting on the cathedral portico? Show my sister some class, Spunner."

"There's no need to play pious, Alex. Eliza and I have a long track record of gambling together." He winked.

"True," Eliza said, "but I don't plan on sitting close enough to read Edmund's expressions. I'll have to pass this time."

"Pity." He took her hand once more. "John is hosting a poker party tonight. Join us, the both of you."

Eliza looked expectantly at Alexander.

"Maybe." He peered around the crowd. "Let's find a seat, Eliza."

"Thank you for the invitation, Sean. I hope to see you later."

Alexander led her to a back pew, and they settled beside each other. Looking at his hands, he spoke in a hushed tone. "You aren't serious about Sean, are you?"

"We have a mutual penchant for fun and games. Nothing more."

"Maybe on your side. I've never seen him so eager to speak with a girl before."

Eliza pinched his leg, and he jerked away. "Don't sound so shocked, brother. I'm a woman now, even if you refuse to see me as such."

He rubbed the spot where she'd pinched him. "I'd have to be blind not to see you as a woman after your escapades last winter."

Eliza went to cover her laugh but clutched his arm instead. "Dear Lord, she's radiant!"

As though knowing of whom she spoke, Alexander focused on a hymnal rather than follow Eliza's line of sight. Lucy came down the side aisle escorted by Frederick, who stopped to speak with someone. The mint green flowered hat that matched her dress perched becomingly on her golden hair. After admiring her glowing countenance, Eliza's gaze roamed Lucy's body. The gathered pleats that curved asymmetrically to a marvelous hip fooled the casual eye with their perceived fullness of fabric, but Eliza knew in an instant the silk could not have created the slight roundness upon Lucy's torso.

"Alex," Eliza hissed. "She looks—"

"Gorgeous," Alex said with bitterness, body rigid as he refused to look. "She's probably with Frederick too. I hear he visits her often."

At that moment, Lucy caught Eliza's stare. Unease marred her eyes—utter heartbreak as Lucy shifted her gaze to Alexander. An ungloved hand went to the pleats on her dress. Frederick spotted the Mellings and hastily escorted Lucy to the front of the nave where the rest of the Eastons sat.

"Oh, Alex. God help you both." Eliza ripped the white mantilla off her head and used it to wipe her tears.

"Eliza," he whispered frantically, "control yourself."

Retrieving a handkerchief, Alexander shoved it into her hand and replaced the mantilla over her hair.

Why hasn't Lucy told him their shared passion created something more than gossip? The combined features of the couple would result in a delicate form of fair beauty. Eliza knew from Lucy's one glance at Alexander that she still desperately loved him. If he knew, he'd do the right thing—of that Eliza was sure. Fatherhood would force him to face his demons with purpose, and he was strong enough to conquer them. *Lucy does him wrong by keeping him in the dark.*

Eliza remained too stunned to think beyond the crushing reality, and Alexander had to tug her upright or to her knees and pull her back onto the pew throughout the ceremony. By the time the wedding was over, Eliza knew it wasn't her place to meddle on Lucy's behalf. Alexander, on the other hand, was fair game.

***

Dr. John Woodslow's poker game might not have been the best place to encourage Alexander to a better life, but it provided plenty of distractions for Eliza from her seat between John and Sean. Alexander sat out the current round, preferring to sprawl on the parlor sofa with a bottle in one hand and his other hand resting on the knee of a woman Eliza had the sneaking suspicion was there as a paid companion to one of the men in attendance—most likely Frank, whom Rupert Lyons had gotten drunk. Eliza listened to the men around the table express their annoyance with Rupert's ways.

Rupert settled between Alexander and the brunette, arm slung about the woman's shoulders as he whispered in her ear.

"And there he goes," John grumbled. "Taking Frank's woman while he's down for the count."

The woman shook her head and glanced at her unresponsive escort in a nearby armchair and then at Alexander, but his eyes were closed.

"Fifteen," she stated.

Sean chuckled. "She's raising her rates on him."

"And how would you know how much she charges?" Eliza countered as she took a drag on a cigarette.

"Men often talk business and finance." Sean winked.

Rupert led the woman toward the hall, but John called him out. "Not in my house, Lyons. Frank wasn't supposed to bring her."

Rupert smirked and pointed to Eliza. "Then why is she here?"

Sean was on his feet in a flash. "Miss Melling is a proper guest."

"She isn't while being the only other female and with no chaperone present," Rupert said.

"She's here with her brother, so shove off."

Rupert left a wake of profanity as he stalked out with the woman.

Eliza smiled at Sean as he returned to his seat. "Well done, Mr. Spunner."

"My pleasure, Eliza." His eyes shone beneath his heavy brow.

"Let's get back to the game," Thomas, sitting across the table, said.

The men's chatter returned with the play.

"You think Eddie's pounded Mary Margaret by now?" Thomas asked.

"He probably got too drunk to complete his husbandly duties," Sean replied.

"No, that's Frank and his penchant for toasting himself out of a lay."

Laughter and more bawdy talk about the possible activities of the newlyweds followed, then Sean changed the subject. "Anyone else notice Grace Anne's change since she returned from Europe? She's more mature."

"You think she got lucky with a Frenchman and won't take kindly to our attentions anymore?" Thomas asked.

"More like what happened with Lucy sobered her," John said. "They always used to go about together."

Alexander straightened on the sofa, leaning toward the table when the name of his beloved was mentioned.

"The golden girls," John continued as he puffed on his cigar. "They're forever tempting us. Alex was bold enough to declare his preference despite Eddie's threats. Who will claim the second?"

"It should be easier since Grace Anne has no brothers," Sean joked.

Thomas laughed. "I've heard she's already been tried out."

John's grip on his cards tightened. "She's a flirt, but not like that."

"Then invite her to our next gathering. She and Eliza can entertain each other when we get too drunk to be proper hosts." Thomas tossed in a few chips.

Eliza added her own bet and a verbal contract. "Plus a kiss for whomever I wish."

"If you lose?" John asked.

She smiled invitingly. "Kissing is a reward, both for me *and* my chosen."

Never had such a poor hand been played by that lot. When Eliza pulled the pile of chips toward her, they all smiled in invitation.

"Everyone push away from the table," she commanded.

As the chairs scraped back, Eliza glanced to Alexander. He clutched the bottle to his chest with both hands, head on the back of the sofa. *Perfect.* She circled the table, her fingers trailing over each man's shoulders as she played her sensual game. On the third pass, she hiked her gown and straddled Sean's lap. Groans of defeat sounded from several of the others as her head tilted toward her playmate.

Sean's hands went to her waist, spreading over the flare of her hips as their lips met, hungry and playful as she ran her tongue over the chipped tooth. Eliza took as much from the moment as possible, reveling in Sean's confident touch and deep kiss while the other men watched. When she felt his manhood rising to the occasion, she brought the display to a close with a final kiss on his scruffy jaw before standing.

"It's been a pleasure, Sean. And thank you for being a lovely host, Dr. Woodslow." She turned to the others. "Gentlemen, I hope to play again with you soon, but I need to get Alexander home before he's too far gone to drive."

Chapter Five

Claudio hurried out to the Mellings when their carriage pulled in front of the church, eager to hear about the wedding they'd attended that week. Kissing Eliza's cheeks, he caressed her lace-gloved hand.

"*Buongiorno*, Eliza."

"Claudio." She purred his name. "You're a picture of virtue this Sabbath morning."

To quiet his yearnings, Claudio looked at Alexander as he exited the carriage. His eyes were bloodshot and smudged with sleeplessness, making him appear as he had the first weekend of their acquaintance—minus the black eye.

"Alexander." Claudio greeted him as always. "I am able to return with you after Mass."

He nodded, his countenance somber. Eliza took them both by an arm and steered them toward the entrance.

"We'll have a lovely afternoon," she said.

The service passed with Claudio daydreaming of Easter Sunday, when Alexander and Eliza had come to the church with their parents for the first time. Claudio had taken Easter dinner with the whole family at Seacliff Cottage and finally understood the bitterness the siblings had for their mother and father. George Melling was an imperious bear and Ruth a plucked chicken, trying to regain her dignity after suffering more than two decades of being dominated by her husband.

When his duties were complete, Claudio gathered with his friends to leave. Alexander curled onto his side the length of one of the carriage benches, forcing the deacon to sit beside Eliza. The fragrance of her rosewater entangled his senses as the press of her shoulder against his arm drove his thoughts to wanting more of her touch.

Eliza raised her lips to his ear, whispering so softly that he had to strain to hear each word in her warm breath. "Alex wishes to speak with you, so I'll go to my room after we eat. Come for me if I'm needed."

He nodded, and Eliza's lips brushed his jaw. Electricity surged from his head to his groin before she leaned away.

At Seacliff Cottage, they gathered at the picnic table on the back porch. His cassock removed, Claudio rolled up his sleeves, blessed the food, then helped himself to the wine that was shared communally. Alexander stayed silent as they ate the cold luncheon. Claudio made small talk with Eliza before she mentioned the poker party she'd attended with Alexander.

"All the men wanted to discuss what the bride and groom might be experiencing that night, but I pitied them both. Mary Margaret has the worst facial structure out of any young lady in the parish, and Edmund—"

"You found unworthy when you gave yourself to him," Alexander said hatefully. "The entire Mystics of Dardenne society knows how unsatisfied you were. But have no fear, little sister. They're all lining up to be the next one for you to try out, and Sean's the most eager."

Eliza jumped up from the table. "You're riddled with pain and want me to be as miserable as you, but that's not going to happen because I know when to quit drinking so that I'm not stumbling around in a drunken haze for days on end! Lucy's never going to come back to you when you look as you do—bloodshot eyes and appearing as though you had two hours sleep in an alley. Not to mention the fact that you can't keep out of the district!"

She ran into the kitchen and up the back stairs.

Claudio put a hand on Alexander's shoulder. "She spoke out of pain, the same as you. But I know you can improve from where you are right now."

Alexander groaned and lay his head onto the table. "I felt Lucy's gaze on me at the wedding. The change in the heavens because we were in the same space was undeniable, but I couldn't raise my head. I'm unworthy to look at her. Those green eyes—how they pierced my soul the moment she turned to me at the Christmas party. God, it hurts to think of it! I wouldn't even let Eliza tell me how she looked."

He straightened enough to drink from the wine bottle, then he tucked his face into the crook of his arm.

Claudio gave him a minute before speaking. "You must slow your drinking, *amico*. It is not good to partake so much."

Alexander shoved the wine at him. "Then you finish it off. I'm not strong enough to turn away from an open bottle."

A third of it was left and Claudio already had a full glass. But to help his friend, the deacon accepted the bottle. Crossing himself, he took a drink.

"Faster!" Alexander urged. "I can smell it and will rip it from your hands to get another swig."

Scared at seeing the mania in Alexander's eyes, Claudio chugged the remainder of the bottle. Setting it down with a clunk, he nodded. "Now what can I do for you? Shall we ride? Walk?"

"My head hurts too much. I'll try to sleep this off."

Claudio saw Alexander to his second floor bedroom then found himself alone in the red hallway. Woozy from drinking the wine so quickly, Claudio braced a hand on the damask wallpaper. In the stillness, a voice like misty rain fell from above.

Eliza sang of heaven with the voice of an angel. He followed the sound up a narrow flight of stairs to an attic room he'd yet to lay eyes upon. What a feast it was! Bold Turkish prints and jeweled colors draped the ceilings and walls as though he'd entered a tent of pleasure. Sitting on a pillow like a princess in the middle of a nest of fabrics, Eliza looked up from the sketchpad on her lap. Her song wavered as she smiled, then she completed the verse and reached a hand toward him.

"Come to me, Claudio. I need to study your profile."

He rounded the low table beside the mountain of pillows. His mouth opened in surprise at the paper before her.

"It is me! You draw well, Eliza."

"My subject is divine." She patted the cushion beside her. "I need to get the line of your jaw exactly right."

He fell on his knees before her. A lily-white hand took his chin and turned his head sideways so he faced a pallet bed adorned in purple silk. Realizing he was alone with Eliza in her chamber, his heart began to race.

"Your room is extraordinary," he said to ease his nerves.

"I put it together for my birthday last year. Easton and Sons imported most of it."

Fabrics were aplenty, but the furnishings were sparse—a teak wardrobe, low table, frameless bed, dresser, writing desk, and an easel by one of the open dormer windows. Otherwise it was a dozen giant pillows thrown about the floor. The warm breeze rustled the drapes so the room resembled a quivering rainbow.

"It is glorious. The perfect space for you." Claudio ached to see if she smiled over his remark but did not wish to earn a reprimand for moving.

Her pencil scratched across the paper for a minute. "There! I just need to check one thing."

Her sketchpad was set aside, then a soft finger touched the bridge of his nose and trailed the slope. With a sharp intake, Claudio held his breath as Eliza's finger traced his lips.

"Your lines are exquisite, Deacon De Fiore. I would draw you all day if I could."

He turned to her when her finger was on the point of his chin. Eliza's eyes burned a deep shade of passion, and her rosy lips beckoned him.

He leaned closer and she withdrew her hand. "I could look upon you always."

Eliza shifted until she perched before him. "Shall we make an arrangement to spend endless days together?"

"One stolen moment and I would be blessed my whole life."

Eliza embraced him with a swiftness that knocked them off balance. They tumbled onto the pile of pillows. Claudio instinctively brought his lips to Eliza's and wrapped her in his arms. Primal hunger drove him in his quest to quench his thirst. Deep, driving kisses and caressing hands ruled the moment.

When he felt the tiny cross she wore on a gold chain about her neck, he jerked to the reality of his situation as though burned by a holy relic.

"Claudio, please don't stop." She snuggled against his chest.

"I am sorry for taking liberties with you, Eliza. I should not have come into your room."

Looking up at him with her luminous eyes, she smiled in her mesmeric way. "I prayed you *would* come."

"I have not held a woman since I started my journey to the priesthood. I am to sacrifice these pleasures so I might better serve the Lord."

"Nothing we do together that brings fulfillment is an abomination, for ours is a God of love. Allow me to show you how magnificent it can be to express these emotions."

She brought him beneath her soft form, settling her hips over his with a delectable grind that spiked his natural man to full attention. The frenzied jumble of fear and want must have registered in his wide eyes, for she kissed him as gently as one would a newborn babe.

"It's all right, Claudio. I'll not go too far. Trust me, my handsome flower."

Eliza kissed from one ear to the other along the line of his jaw with teasing nips. He grasped her hips and pressed upward to feel her center while he nestled into her neck and hair. Then their mouths were upon the other once more, focusing his rebirth into a life of carnal appetites.

When he grew concerned over losing control, Claudio rolled them onto their sides and kissed Eliza's nose to break the spell.

"You bring me such joy," she whispered. "Thank you."

He smoothed her dark locks. "Do you need me?"

"I need you to feel loved, appreciated, and alive."

"Then I will be here for you, Eliza." His grin reflected back in her bright smile.

SUMMER

Chapter Six

Eliza woke in the June heat from another impassioned dream about Claudio. She had visited Seacliff Cottage with Alexander twice since the event with the deacon in her bedroom, but never were they alone together. This afternoon, all the Mellings were taking the ferry across the bay to set up summer residence. The men would continue to commute more often than not during the week, but it was the first year without a governess in attendance, and the thought of alone time with her mother did not excite Eliza. Teas at the hotel in Point Clear would be the norm at least twice a week, along with dances and socials while the Mobile elite escaped the heat of the city during the balmy weather. She hoped Alexander would still regularly host the deacon to break the monotony.

Eliza's morning routine ended when she twisted her hair into a loose bun. She hurried downstairs in a thin wash dress she often wore when painting. Her father sat behind the newspaper at the head of the massive dining table, steam from his coffee cup billowing in the breeze from the open French doors.

"Good morning, Father."

"Did the maids help you pack?"

"We finished Wednesday. The driver took Mother's and my luggage to the ferry yesterday afternoon so we aren't burdened with it today."

The paper rustled as he turned a page. "And Seacliff was notified?"

"Mr. Campbell and Mr. Watts were to meet the ferry to collect everything."

"Good."

Eliza lifted the silver lid keeping the pancake platter warm and piled four onto her plate. Settling with her favorite breakfast, she hastily crossed herself before eating.

Alexander entered without a word. He nodded at his sister and helped himself to coffee and grits. Knowing he didn't wish to draw their father's attention, Eliza only smiled in return.

Then their mother arrived. Immaculately dressed in a dove gray ensemble with not a hair out of place on her brunette pompadour, her sharp eyes took in the sight of her family as she paused behind her chair.

"On your feet this instant, Eliza."

She quickly obeyed, already knowing the faults Ruth would find in her appearance.

"It's completely improper to come to the table like that. Anyone could stop in and see you unbound in that homely sack with your hair in disarray."

"No one ever stops in during breakfast, Mother."

"Watch your tone, young lady." George lowered his newspaper. "Though you're quite right. It's a shame your mother pushes corsets on you when your natural shape is young and firm. Corsets are for old ladies and evening affairs."

"Well!" Ruth huffed and sat stiffly in her chair. "At the rate she eats, I will soon be unable to squeeze her into anything."

"I have no complaints about my figure, Mother. In fact, many of Alexander's friends can't keep their eyes off me."

George gave a hearty laugh and stroked his mustache. "That's my daughter—the belle of the ball. So long as they fill their needs elsewhere and not at your table, it's all well and good. A true gentleman knows better than to tarnish a debutante. I hope Alex learned his lesson."

Red-faced, Alexander pushed back from the table with enough force to topple the cream. "Don't speak of anything to do with my Lucy!"

"She's not yours, even if you took her innocence," George said. "The whole town is talking about how Frederick Davenport calls at the Eastons practically every night. Whose lips do you think Lucille is kissing now, boy?"

With a growling roar more suited to a menagerie, Alexander sprang. George caught him across the jaw with the back of his hand.

Stumbling against the nearest dining chair, Alexander barely stayed upright.

"Be a man, Alexander."

"A man like you, Father? One who makes sure his sexual needs are fed *appropriately* with liaisons? One who takes his son to a whorehouse to welcome him into adulthood and provides him with an allowance for regular visits from then on?"

Ruth paled and looked unable to speak as George advanced with another strike at Alexander.

"I'm despicable, aren't I?" Alexander shouted. "Thank you, *Father*, for my wonderful upbringing. I wouldn't be the failure at relationships that I am without your guidance." He dealt an icy glare to George then abruptly left.

Caught between cheering for her brother's bold words and pitying the blows he'd been dealt, Eliza silently watched him go.

Ruth looked at her husband. "Geor—"

"Shut up!" He swept his plate to the floor, grimacing over the shattered china. "I'll not discuss a word of his unrealistic accusations! I've done all I can to educate him on the ways of the world to no avail. That simpleton is no son of mine!"

As soon as he stormed out, Ruth began to cry. Not wishing to stay in the uncomfortable scene, Eliza stood to go.

"Where do you think you are going?" Ruth swiped her cheeks with a lace-trimmed handkerchief. "You haven't finished your breakfast."

"I wish to paint while the morning light is good," Eliza replied. "Besides, you've already said I eat too much."

"Don't leave me."

"I'll be back to take dinner with you, Mother."

Eliza stole through the kitchen without a word to the cook, rushing across the lawn and out of the gate to the detached garage at the end of the driveway. The stairs within the simple structure led to a two-room apartment she used as an art studio. She immediately set to work mixing colors for the oil painting she was in the middle of creating. Working from a photograph, she stood at the easel to complete the image of the front of the mansion her insufferable parents had built. All morning, Eliza tried to capture a sense of light within the house of sorrow. Maybe someday a family would fill the space with love.

***

On the way to the dock, Ruth stopped at the drugstore so she could purchase something for her nerves. Eliza waited in the back of the limousine, gazing at the office front of Easton and Sons a few doors down. A minute later, Lucy emerged on her eldest brother's arm. She looked surprisingly trim compared to her state at Edmund's wedding the month before.

Maxwell walked Lucy to the nearest trolley stop and waited with her. Eliza noticed that most of the people who passed them stared, and those walking with someone else leaned together to whisper. Lucy shifted nervously, but Maxwell kept by her side, holding her arm. He stayed until the streetcar pulled away with his sister onboard before heading for his office.

Eliza jumped out of the automobile. "Mr. Easton!"

Turning toward Eliza's voice, Maxwell looked surprised. "Miss Melling?"

She smiled in relief over his acknowledgment and careened to a stop before him on the sidewalk. "How's Lucy? She looks well, but is she?"

His hazel eyes were kind compared to Edmund's harsh stare, though Eliza was sure they could be just as cutting if he were upset. His chin angled down as he replied, "She's had a rough go of it these past months, but I was able to talk her into taking dinner with me. This was her first time out of the house since Eddie's wedding. We dined at the Trellis Room then came back here for coffee to escape the curious stares."

"I'm glad she has you, Mr. Easton. And Mr. Davenport. I hear he visits often."

Maxwell's smile was bitter. "She has at least one true friend in Freddy."

"I'd visit her if I thought I'd be welcomed."

He nodded and turned as though wishing to leave. "It was nice to—"

Eliza took his arm. "She has no health complaints?"

"Beyond a broken heart? No, Miss Melling. Thank you for asking after her, but I won't pass along to her that you did. You understand, don't you?"

"Yes. Thank you for giving me a minute of your time." She watched him retreat until he disappeared within the doorway to his office.

Settled back inside the automobile, Eliza blinked away tears. She doubted Lucy's family even knew of her pregnancy—and mysterious loss—since she hadn't been sent away. Would she ever accept Alexander back after going through such pain?

The ferry ride across the bay was fraught with ill-concealed anger and pain from everyone. Eliza's parents refused to make eye contact with each other, but the blaring absence of Alexander hurt her most. She paced the upper deck, white dress billowing in the warm wind. As they approached the first stop, Eliza looked toward the Daphne pier. Alexander stood beside Claudio, who looked regal in his black cassock in the afternoon sun.

As soon as the deckhands had the gangplank secure, Eliza rushed into her brother's arms and kissed his bruised jaw. "I don't blame you for leaving this morning, Alex."

"I rode a fishing boat across and found Claudio."

"Dear Claudio!" Eliza kissed his cheeks. "Thank you for caring for him."

"It is my pleasure to help a friend in need."

"He's coming over tomorrow," Alexander said. "We're going to ride and picnic if you'd like to join us, Eliza."

"Of course!" She took her brother's arm.

Alexander turned to the deacon. "Thank you again."

Claudio smiled. "I will see you both tomorrow."

Eliza led Alexander onto the ferry. "We'll stay topside, away from Father and Mother. They're not speaking to each other."

"I'm sick of his lies and manipulation."

"I know."

They settled on a bench on the top deck, Eliza resting her head on Alexander's shoulder.

"No matter what happens with our parents, I won't forsake you, Alex. Will you be here for me as well?"

"Only if you promise to keep away from Claudio."

She giggled and fingered the cross at her neck. "I can't swear to that."

"He's a man of God, Eliza. Tread carefully. Your prowess is becoming legendary."

"They're all just a bit of fun. Nothing serious and they know it."

"I wouldn't be so sure, Eliza Rose."

Chapter Seven

Summer became Claudio's favorite

season. Weekend ramblings with Alexander and Eliza, which
sometimes extended into formal suppers at Seacliff Cottage with their
parents, were blessed times. In addition, Eliza often rode Flora to
Daphne during the week, stopping by to talk or work beside him
while he labored in the churchyard. Then they would walk to
Jackson's Oak while they spoke of everything that moved them. So
familiar was he becoming with their relaxed hours together—for he
was without his cassock when riding and working outdoors—he felt
constrained in his vestments when he saw her across the chapel on
Sundays.

On the Fourth of July, Claudio made arrangements to meet
Alexander and Eliza early that Tuesday morning so they could spend
the whole day together. He was offered a lift in a wagon heading to
Fairhope and disembarked at the lane to Seacliff Cottage. Not
wanting to disturb the household, he went to the stables to greet the
horses.

Eliza sat with a sketchpad on the saddle stool across from
Flora's open stall. Her blue-and-white striped dress was a simple
cotton frock, unlike any he had seen her in. Her posture relaxed
without shapewear, she hunched over her work in a natural state. She
drew for another minute before looking at the doorway and tucking
her pencil behind her ear.

"Claudio!"

He went to her open arms, kissing each cheek as she did the
same. Then Eliza's arms were around his neck, keeping him leaning

over her so she could kiss his mouth. The exquisite torture he had waited months to feel again set his body on fire. Eliza opened the buttons on the top half of his cassock. She revealed his shirt and tucked two fingers into his waistband, teasing for a forbidden touch.

"No, Eliza. We cannot do more."

"There's so much to share."

He kissed her forehead and stepped out of her embrace. "I do not wish to bring punishment upon your beautiful soul."

"It's a sin to leave me feeling alone in this cruel world." The pain in her bright eyes brought him back to her.

"I would give you all if I could, *la mia Rose*." Holding her tight, he trailed kisses across her face.

Alexander's voice came from the house's back porch. "Eliza, I want to leave as soon as I gather the picnic!"

They stepped away from each other, Claudio finishing the removal of his cassock. Eliza stashed her art supplies into a satchel and saddled Flora.

Claudio hung his frock and greeted Alexander while Eliza emerged from Flora's stall. After Alexander secured their picnic bag—twice as large as typical—he mounted Janus.

"I have a friend meeting us by the pier in Fairhope, so let's be off." Alexander spurred Janus toward the path.

"See, even my brother doesn't find fault in our ways. He accepts that we ride together." Eliza handed Flora's bridle to Claudio.

"He objected the first time, though he knows how stubborn you are and chose not to fight you over it." He mounted the horse, careful of the baggage.

Eliza smiled as she pulled up the hem of her cotton dress. Beginning at the bottom, she undid the buttons on the front of her dress until she reached the area of her lap. Flipping the sides back as though they were coattails, she displayed an expanse of white underdrawers that ended in a row of ruffles above her bare knees. Then she was behind him, pale legs squeezing the outside of his trousers with tempting strength.

Eliza's heels brought Flora to action, following the trail Alexander blazed to the beach. It was a blessing the horse knew the way because Claudio could do little more than hold the reins while the temptress behind him skimmed her hands down his back and around his chest with a seductive touch. No thick riding habit or stiff corset separated them. Her soft breasts pressed against his back as her hands continued to explore.

When Alexander saw them emerge from the trees, he galloped southward. Eliza used their privacy to pull Claudio's shirt free so she could spread her fingers across the skin beneath it. He shuddered under her touch when she kissed his ear.

"I know you want me as much as I do you, Claudio."

He slowed Flora at the words and leaned against Eliza's soft curves. As though seeking to use the change of pace to her advantage, she spread her palms against his chest and trailed them down—waist, hips, upper thighs. His body happily responded with the call of the natural man.

"Please, Eliza. We must not—"

Her right hand shot back beneath his shirt and pinched a nipple. Claudio yelped and jerked forward, setting Flora to a faster trot.

"I am trying to protect you," he said over his shoulder.

"I don't wish protection from my muse. I need to be possessed by passion!" She nudged Flora's flanks.

Feeling her heart pounding against his back as the horse raced across the sand, Claudio did his best to quiet the longings seeking to undo him. Their horse overtook Alexander, and soon after Claudio stopped under the public pier. He quickly dismounted before Eliza could sway him to other matters with her roaming hands.

With a haunting look, she slid into the prominent saddle position and set Flora circling him. "I'm disappointed, Claudio. I thought we had an understanding. I thought I meant something to you."

Before he could respond, Alexander came to an abrupt halt beside them.

"Is a lady friend joining us, Alex?" Eliza asked. "Do I get to play chaperone for you?"

He shook his head and Claudio stepped close enough to stroke Janus. "Then I am to meet one of your city friends?"

"Yes, he's here for the holiday—Sean Spunner."

Eliza laughed, the smile reaching her bright eyes. "My favorite Dardenne! Despite the rocky start, this will be a fun day. Thank you, Alex. I'll gladly accept your offering."

"Tread carefully, Eliza Rose. He likes you."

"And I like him. He's such fun!" She slipped off Flora, her open dress slow to follow her descent.

"Eliza, button your gown!"

"I forgot to change and I need it like this to ride astride."

A horse whinnied from nearby and Claudio turned. A young man in riding breeches with a white shirt and a brown Western hat trotted up to the group on a glossy black horse. Glancing at Eliza, Claudio felt the stab of jealousy over her true smile as she approached the newcomer.

"Alex just told me you were joining us, Sean. I'm glad to see you. You look dashing."

He smoothly dismounted and kept a firm hold on the bridle as he took Eliza's hand with his other. "Mobile isn't the same without the Mellings. Forgive me for not removing my hat, but I don't wish to let this borrowed stallion go without knowing his full temperament, nor do I ever wish to lose your touch."

She giggled at his suave words and matched the spark in his eyes with her own fire. She snatched the hat from his head with her free hand and used it to shield them from Alexander as she kissed him. "I'll take good care of you today, Sean. May I ride with you?"

"Introductions first, Eliza," Alexander reprimanded.

"It's only Claudio."

Her dismissive words twisted the knife of envy within Claudio's heart. Alexander frowned at her, and she shifted into a moody stance.

"Hold his horse a moment, Eliza." Alexander motioned Claudio over to Sean. "Sean, this is Deacon Claudio De Fiore with The Church of the Assumption in Daphne. He's training to be a priest. Claudio, my good friend and fellow lawyer, Sean Spunner."

"A man of the cloth, Alex?" Sean said. "How handy that must make it for confessions to have one with you." He turned back to help Eliza into his saddle and swung up behind her, arms immediately about her waist as he smiled at Claudio. "Do stay close, Deacon De Fiore. I might have need of confession before noon."

Eliza leaned against him and laughed, but she was not catty enough to look at Claudio to see if she was getting to him. She appeared genuinely pleased with her new companion. Part of Claudio wanted to be happy for her, but the louder voice wanted to strike the man and stomp his perfect American hat.

Claudio and Alexander returned to their horses and followed Eliza's lead. Sean appeared all too happy to allow her to take control, for it freed his arms to stay snugly about her middle.

Alexander kept beside Claudio. "Don't look so put out, Deacon. Someone might get the idea you fancy my sister."

"Is he to be trusted?"

Alexander laughed. "He's a Mystics of Dardenne member, though he and his friend John are more respectable than most. They rarely enter the district outside of Mardi Gras, if that's what you mean."

"She deserves to be more than a conquest."

A bitter scowl shadowed Alexander's face. "She's no innocent, though she's not much older than a child."

"Eliza is—"

"I know she's led you on from time to time, but please don't judge my sister too harshly today. I think this time with Sean will be good for her. Perhaps it will force her to grow up and possibly settle down."

"She is young. There is plenty of time for her to settle in life."

Alexander reached Claudio's arm and gripped it, fear displayed on his pale complexion. "She mustn't make the same mistakes I've made. Please guide her away from that path."

"*Sí, amico.* I will do all I can to bring her to repentance when necessary."

"Thank you, Claudio." Alexander released his hold. "Sean would be a good match for her. I bet Father would even bring him into the firm, not that I'd wish that upon him. God knows the further away from George Melling you can be, the better."

Alexander spurred Janus into a gallop. Not wanting to be left behind, Claudio urged Flora to follow.

Chapter Eight

Alexander thundered past on Janus.

"Shall we race him?" Sean asked.

Eliza rested her head against his chest. "I rather like this pace for now."

"I've missed you, Eliza." He nipped her ear and raised himself to lean over her shoulder. "You've spoiled me for any other company at poker games and balls. And we can now add riding to that list. I've never seen such an erotic sight as your legs spanning this horse."

"He's a fine stallion. What's his name and where did you get him?"

"Bruiser is his name, from a stable south of Fairhope. My uncle rents from it when we're on this side of the bay."

Eliza leaned forward to whisper in the horse's ear and stroked his gleaming black neck. Sean's hands trailed to Eliza's hips, teasing her bunched dress around her upper thighs. The sound of Flora approaching triggered a flutter in her stomach and she straightened. When Claudio rode past, she waved and smiled around the pain of his rebuke, then she settled her hand on Sean's knee and turned a cheek to him.

"Explore if you'd like," she said. "I've told Bruiser to keep steady, and he promised not to throw us if we get exuberant."

"There's no one like you." Sean kissed her temple as his hands smoothed down either leg until he struck the skin below her ruffled drawers. His warm hands caressed the flesh above her knees, thumbs working the fabric higher with each movement. He hadn't explored as far as Eliza wished when his hands returned to her middle. Begging for more attention, she arched against him, and he needed no encouragement in what to do. His hands trailed up her sides and cupped her breasts in a firm squeeze that pulled a whimper of satisfaction from her lips.

"Eliza, you're extraordinary."

She shifted sideways, and her lips went to his with hunger. They carried on until Bruiser cantered to a stop.

She laughed and slipped from the horse. "I'm used to Flora. She knows my ramblings and will follow Janus without instructions. Take the reins so I can relax."

Sean shifted to the front of the saddle. "Are you often preoccupied on Flora? Did you sit with the deacon before I arrived?"

"I usually daydream about something when riding. And yes, I was with Claudio."

"Riding with Alex would give you more room since he's smaller."

"What woman would choose to ride with her brother over a handsome Italian?" Eliza snuggled on the saddle behind Sean. "Shall I show you what I did to the deacon to try to sway him?"

Laughing, Sean set the horse back to a trot. "You wicked woman. Show me everything."

Untucking his shirt from his breeches, Eliza's hands explored up the inside of his clothing. Sean was more masculine feeling than Edmund and firmer than Claudio. His pectoral muscles were covered with soft hair, and the desire to draw him filled her mind.

Sean laid a hand on her bare knee. "Mmm, you tortured the poor man."

Eliza giggled and snaked her hands into position to pinch his nipples.

He shouted a curse—startling Bruiser into breaking his stride—but then immediately laughed. "I'll get you back when you least expect it, Miss Melling."

"I hope so." She smiled and rested her cheek against his back while linking her hands about his waist.

They made a brief stop at Zundel's, where Alexander bought a few more supplies for their day before continuing south. After tethering the horses in a shady spot off the narrow road that led west along the peninsula to Fort Morgan, Eliza allowed Sean to carry her satchel and took his arm for the trek across the glaring white sand toward the Gulf of Mexico. Claudio and Alexander followed with the picnic supplies.

They settled their blanket on the deserted stretch of beach a dozen feet from the shoreline. Alexander immediately opened a bottle of wine and another of brandy, offering them to Sean. He took the brandy and Alexander passed the wine to Claudio. Hoping to keep as much of the brandy from her brother as possible, Eliza cuddled beside Sean and they passed the bottle several times while he removed his boots.

"Save some for me, Spunner." Alexander plopped onto the blanket on the opposite side of Eliza. When he took the brandy, he inhaled the aroma then chugged.

"I forgot how you love your drink, Melling," Sean said.

Eliza took the bottle back from Alexander and looked at Claudio. "Please join us."

He lifted the wine bottle. "Then I would have to share this."

"The four of us share everything today." Eliza smiled and patted the space in front of her.

Claudio parked himself there, but Sean put an arm around Eliza and kissed her cheek.

"There's one delicious treat I don't wish to share with anyone else."

Warmth flooded her center as she looked at him. Charming, sweet, and naughty—there was no doubt Sean was all three, but Claudio's earnestness beckoned her almost as strongly.

"Come on, pass it back," Alexander said.

Fortunately, Sean took another swig before passing along the half-empty bottle.

Alexander partook heavily then jumped to his feet and began pulling off his clothes until only his underdrawers remained.

Sean whistled and clapped. "Thanks for the show, Melling, but I'd prefer it to be your sister down to her undies."

"That could be arranged," Eliza said with a smile. "I'm halfway there already."

He grinned and fingered her knee that peeked through the open dress. "You tease."

Alexander ran for the water and dove in once he was waist deep.

"Is he a strong swimmer?" Claudio asked Eliza, though he kept his eyes on Alexander in the surf.

"Average, but he never goes far from shore. Join him if you'd like, Claudio. I know you're worried after he drank so much."

"*Sí*, I will."

Claudio pulled off his shoes and socks before standing. Eliza couldn't help but stare as he opened his shirt and removed his trousers—olive skin dark against the white sand and bright blue sky. He caught her gaze when he folded his pants to leave them on the blanket.

"You'll allow me to draw you, won't you, Claudio?"

He shook his head and went for the water without a word.

"And what of me, Eliza?" Sean's smile dimpled his left cheek, and his eyes shone amber in the late morning sun.

She pounced on him, knocking his hat off as she pushed him back and straddled his lap. "I'd do more than draw you, Sean Spunner."

Lips surging together, Eliza gloried in her dominant stance even as he took control from below. His hands went under her dress, grasping her hips to move her against him in a playful cadence that had her wanting their clothing removed. Eliza opened his shirt, kissing a trail down from his neck as his skin was revealed.

She pulled the shirt off his arms and jumped up. With a tilted head she studied him, from his bulging breeches to his heavy brows. "Yes, Mr. Spunner. You'd do nicely to draw as well."

"You minx!" He laughed and pulled her into his arms as he stood.

Eliza couldn't help running her hands over his firm torso. "Do you box?"

"I prefer the punching bag and weights, but I get in the ring often enough to be reminded why I stay out." In answer to her questioning look, he pointed to his tooth. "Injuries. I'm used to striking a bag and forget to keep my guard up."

"Have you ever gone against Frederick Davenport?"

"He nearly busted my ribs a few months back. I haven't climbed through the ropes since. I think he was taking out his frustrations over Alex on me since I'm friends with the man who ruined Lucy. Why? Is he someone you'd like to draw?"

"As a matter of fact, I would. But I'd have a better chance getting the deacon disrobed than sitting in the same room as Frederick." She rested her cheek against Sean's chest, enjoying the warmth and security she felt.

He kissed the top of her head. "Davenport has mellowed the past month or two. I suppose that means he's getting in good with Lucy. She was always a sweet girl. I remember a couple of big rows Eddie had at their house when we were kids. Back then I had my eyes on the Easton twins, but little Lucy played with the boys. She would scout from Eddie's tree fort while the battle raged on the ground. Whichever team she aided always won."

"Let me guess—Frederick's?"

He lifted her chin and flashed his chipped-tooth smile. "Yes, but I'd go to the ring to win your approval."

"You already have it."

She'd never seen such adoration in a man as she did that moment. A lock of murky brown hair fell over his eye, reminding Eliza how she'd found that shade intolerable as recent as that winter. But he did look dashing in a hat—and without a shirt. Sean was excitement and fun, sensual and carefree while still being thoughtful.

Why shouldn't I allow him to sweep me off my feet?

"How about a swim, Eliza?"

She nodded as the others returned.

"I hope you two didn't drink the rest of the brandy." Alexander shook his head to clear the water from his hair, raining droplets on the romantic moment. Then he collapsed on the blanket and chugged from the bottle. Belching long and loud, he nodded to Sean. "Have you felt her up yet, Spunner? Do I need to challenge you to defend her honor? Oh, that's right. My sister threw that way when she and Eddie copulated at his bachelor party."

Sean's lip curved with amused scorn. "You were going at *his* sister at the same time, so come off your high horse."

Alexander fell back on the blanket, wet underwear clinging to his thin legs. "I'll sleep it off."

Claudio looked at Eliza and whispered. "I will watch him."

There was pain in his dark eyes, but she didn't know if it was over Alexander's behavior or the words he'd spoken about her. Eliza rested her hand on his bare arm and gazed with supplicating eyes. "I could stay with you."

Claudio shook his head and looked away. "Go with your friend. We shall eat when you return."

Swallowing her misgivings, Eliza turned to Sean with a saucy smile. "Still ready for that swim, Mr. Spunner?"

He bit his lip as his hands went to his belt, the amber fire in his eyes intense.

Eliza opened the remaining buttons on her cotton dress and draped it over Alexander's slumbering body. She met Claudio's gaze—which stayed at her eye level despite the fact that only a thin layer of white cotton concealed her curves. "Keep him covered, Claudio. He's prone to sunburns."

"*Sí*, Eliza."

Sean took her hand. "You have a nurturing spirit."

"Someone needs to protect him. Lord knows our parents never coddled us." Seeing the worry on his face, Eliza was quick to smile. "He'll be fine. Come on!"

She led him down the beach several dozen feet before splashing into the Gulf because she didn't want to flaunt their actions directly in front of Claudio.

Once they were waist deep in the water, Sean reached around to pinch her as she'd done to him. Eliza shrieked and flailed to get some distance between them before turning.

His eyes were on her chemisette. The wet ruffles did little to hide her chest. "My God, you're flawless."

"Are you going to turn our sinful behavior into a religious experience?"

Sean splashed her to drench the fabric further and raised his arms in praise. "I hear a host of heavenly angels singing the glories of your perfect tits, Eliza Melling! You'll be worth going to the confessional. Every damn time."

Laughing, she fell against Sean. His playful touches chased her cares away as the sun warmed her skin amid the turquoise water surrounding them.

Chapter Nine

Claudio did his best not to watch Eliza's antics, but as the minutes crawled by under the summer sun, she and Sean drifted in front of the picnic spot. They played while Claudio's heart bled through to his soul.

Alexander moaned and rolled to his side. A second later, he jerked upright, pushing Eliza's dress off of him. "What happened?"

"You drank too much brandy, and your sister is entertaining your guest." Claudio motioned to the surf where Sean had Eliza in a rapturous hold while they kissed.

Alexander tucked his knees to his bare chest and hugged them. "What I wouldn't have done to have a moment like that with Lucy, but it wasn't feasible with our winter courtship."

"It does not bother you to see her engaged as such?"

Alexander snorted a laugh and turned to Claudio. "It obviously bothers you. Will you call them to repentance when they emerge?"

"You did ask me to help keep Eliza on the right path."

"But also to allow her this day with no judgment. Sean is good for her."

"*Sí*, she appears happy." *Too happy.*

"Don't sound so heartbroken, Claudio. You swore off women when you joined the priesthood."

Eliza refused to dress until her undergarments dried, so every peak, valley, and detail was displayed through the clinging white fabric. In true Eliza fashion, she did nothing to attempt a semblance of modesty. Everyone joked and talked during the torturous picnic, except Claudio.

Once Eliza finally buttoned the top of her dress, Alexander made a brotherly comment. "I bet you're glad I'm not a fighter, Spunner. You'd be fifteen shades of blue by now if I were."

Sean laughed. "Praise the Lord for small miracles."

Eliza looked at the man with unveiled longing as Alexander packed the remainders.

"May I have the wine bottle?" Sean approached Alexander while Claudio and Eliza folded the blanket.

"It's empty."

"That's why I want it." He turned to Eliza. "Would you be willing to part with a piece of paper from your sketch pad?"

"A message in a bottle?" Her blue-violet eyes brightened when he nodded. "How clever!"

She leaned over his shoulder as he wrote with one of her pencils. Giggling, she snatched the note from him when he was done and waved it before Alexander and Claudio. Her brother grabbed it and held it steady so they could read.

> *On the glorious Day of Independence, July 4, 1905, four souls gathered on the white sands of Alabama. Food and libations were part of their escapades. But do not worry for the sake of their souls. One of them—a man of the cloth— watched as a shepherd over the wayward flock of frolicking Catholics. And only two partook of slightly debauched activities. Join us next year east of Fort Morgan to witness our merry krewe.*
> *Yours in revelry,*
> *Mystics of Dardenne and guests*

Alexander doubled over with laughter while Sean rolled the paper to fit into the bottle's opening. Cork in place, he threw the glass beyond the breaking waves. They watched in silence as the written confession floated out to sea.

Eliza took Sean around his waist. "Will you really return next year?"

"Only if you promise to join me."

"I do!"

Eliza turned away too quickly to see the effect those two simple words had on Sean, but Claudio would have sworn that the man swooned.

***

The trip north was impossibly long, but after saying goodbye to Sean at the Fairhope pier, Eliza settled on Flora behind Claudio.

"Did you like him?" She swirled a finger along Claudio's forearm below his rolled sleeves.

"*Sí*, he is good company and makes you happy."

Eliza sighed and rubbed her cheek on Claudio's back. "He does and is willing to indulge me, unlike a certain friend this morning."

"I told you it is not good for us, Eliza, but I am glad you had a splendid time despite your perceived setback."

Mr. and Mrs. Melling were sitting in the rocking chairs on the back porch when the group rode into the stable yard.

"Eliza Rose!" Mrs. Melling called as soon as her daughter touched the ground. "What in heaven's name are you wearing?"

She turned away long enough to fasten a few more buttons before calling to her mother. "I need to care for Flora!"

Mrs. Melling came to the back gate to get a better look. "Let Alexander or Mr. Campbell see to that while you come here and explain why you left the house looking like a washer woman!"

"Save me, Claudio," she whispered.

Crossing himself, he dismounted. "I shall do what I can to ease her wrath," he whispered in return.

Mrs. Melling smiled in welcome. "Deacon De Fiore, it is always a blessing to have you here. I must apologize for the state of my daughter. Had I known she was dressed as such, I never would have let her out the door this morning. Eliza, where on earth did you even get a hold of something like that?"

"It's one of my painting frocks, Mother. It was too hot to wear a riding habit when we were gone all day to the Gulf."

"The three of you went all the way to the Gulf?" Mrs. Melling shook her head. "Such a waste when there are excellent people in Fairhope and Point Clear for the holiday."

"We weren't alone," Alexander said as he came up behind them. "We met my friend Sean in Fairhope. He journeyed with us."

Mr. Melling stood as the others stepped onto the porch. "Sean Spunner joined you?"

"Yes, sir."

Mr. Melling smoothed his mustache and looked down his nose at Alexander. "Now, he's a credit to the profession. I saw him in court last week, yelling at the defendant like a Pentecostal preacher during a tent revival. Yet, at the Aethelwulf Club, he gets the men laughing like nobody else."

"Why did you not bring him here, Alexander?" Mrs. Melling asked. "How long is he staying on this side of the bay?"

"Through the week at the Grand Hotel. We were all a bit rough from the ride, Mother, and a gentleman like him would not wish to appear unkempt when calling on the lady of a house."

Mrs. Melling clasped her hands. "I must send him an invitation to supper on a night he is free. Will you dine with us tonight, Claudio?"

"*Sí*, I would enjoy that. I must wash up and fetch my cassock from the stable."

"Two hours is plenty of time for all of you to prepare for supper. Eliza, I expect you to be properly attired when you enter the dining room."

Claudio washed then waited for Alexander at his writing desk. Eliza came and went from her private bath down the hall. Stopping in the door to her brother's room, she leaned against the frame, a bathrobe tied about her waist and her hair in a wet braid.

"Tell Alexander I'm sorry, but I can't go to the supper table tonight."

"Why not, Eliza Rose?" Alexander nudged her into his room as he entered wearing only a towel about his middle.

She flopped into the armchair by the unlit fireplace. "I don't want my perfect day spoiled by Mother's incessant nagging or Father's superior attitude."

Alexander pulled on a pair of drawers underneath his towel. "And you don't wish to wear a corset after your day of freedom."

Laughing, she looked at Claudio as Alexander dropped his towel on the floor and tugged on navy trousers. "It was wonderful when riding. Don't you think so, Claudio?"

Face heating, Claudio looked to the floor. "It was a new experience."

"One you enjoyed?" She raised her eyebrows teasingly.

"You are a beautiful woman, Eliza, but it is not for me to seek your wonders."

Alexander fell back on his bed with a laugh. "I think Claudio is trying to cover something while Eliza wishes it bared."

"There's no need for confession from me today." Eliza coyly played with the tip of her braid as though it were a paintbrush adding color to her cheek.

"I saw you in the water with Sean when I woke from my nap." Alexander rolled to his stomach and gave her the Melling stare across the room. "You don't know how lucky you are with me as a brother."

"Oh, I know, Alex." She sashayed across the room to kiss his forehead. "I'll come to supper if you promise me a bonfire afterward, the both of you."

Alexander caught Claudio's eye, and he nodded in agreement. He turned to his sister. "Be sure to lace your corset properly, young lady."

Chapter Ten

The bonfire was a dreamy way to end the day. Eliza leaned against Claudio while Alexander lamented over Lucy. They passed a bottle around until Alexander looked ready to shatter. Then Eliza and Claudio helped him to bed. After rousing Mr. Campbell to take Claudio home in the carriage, they stood together by the white picket fence.

"Will you come to tea Thursday?" Eliza asked, knowing Alexander would be in Mobile and her parents were attending a gathering at the hotel.

"*Sí*, it is a joy to spend time with your family while you are here."

"We need you, Claudio." She kissed his cheeks in farewell as the carriage rolled to a stop beside them.

He kissed her in return. "*Arrivederci*, Eliza."

She spent the following day in her attic room, trying to capture on canvas the blues of the Gulf she and Sean had played in the day before. An hour after suffering through the midday dinner, her mother climbed the attic stairs waving a letter.

"Mr. Spunner has accepted the invitation. He would like to join us Thursday evening. Alexander will take the ferry to the hotel, and Mr. Campbell will meet them both there. To return the favor, Mr. Spunner would like to host us at the hotel for supper and dancing on Saturday. Allow me to choose your clothing for both meals."

Knowing Sean wouldn't care what she wore because he had the vision of her in the waves wearing nothing but her clinging undergarments, Eliza ignored her mother's fussing about her limited wardrobe while she kept mixing blue and yellow until the oils created the perfect shade for the crest of a wave.

"The pink gown will do for Thursday, but I'll telegram the mansion for the maid to send over your blue silk for Saturday. That shows off your chest to its best advantage."

Eliza smiled wickedly at the thought of Sean's praise over her breasts. "I'm sure Sean will appreciate that, Mother."

"All men do. Never forget that."

First thing Thursday morning, Alexander took the ferry to the city to work for the day—at least that's what he told the family. Eliza had the sneaking suspicion he would be in the district, keeping company with one of his women. Their parents left at ten for a brunch in Point Clear, followed by some social gatherings that would keep them away all afternoon. Eliza hurried about once they rode away in the carriage. Wearing another simple cotton dress, she pulled her hair into a loose chignon and descended the stairs.

Rosemary and Leroy were straightening the parlor, their tiny daughter, Priscilla, sitting on the rug with a ragdoll.

"Would you like some eggs, Miss Eliza?" Rosemary asked.

She smiled at the cook's kindness, for Eliza knew her mother had given Rosemary instructions to feed her nothing but broth the next two days.

"I'll fix myself some buttered bread, but thank you. I have a guest coming for tea, so you could prepare a few sandwiches and dessert."

"Of course, Miss Eliza."

"You can go on errands if needed after it's fixed. Unlike my brother, I know how to boil water."

Rosemary laughed. "We'll see how it all works out this afternoon. I do need a few things from the market to finish supper preparations."

Eliza sliced two pieces off the loaf on the cutting board and slathered them liberally with the honey butter her mother tried to hide. She took her bread and a cup of milk outside to her favorite rock on the cliff. Eating while she daydreamed of Sean, she absentmindedly watched the boats in the bay. Afterward, she spent a few hours at her easel.

When she descended the stairs later, Eliza found Rosemary setting a platter into the icebox.

"I didn't fix too many. We don't want leftovers around when your mother returns."

"Thank you, Rosemary."

"I'll be back to finish supper in an hour or so."

After the Watts family left in their wagon, Eliza waited for Claudio's arrival in the shade of the front porch with her sketchbook. He soon meandered up the lane in the summer humidity.

She jumped to her bare feet. "Good afternoon, Claudio! Hurry in and remove your cassock so you can cool off."

"*Buongiorno*, Eliza." His hand went to her shoulder when they kissed cheeks.

She took his arm and brought him into the crimson parlor. After setting her sketchbook on the coffee table, she pointed at the settee. "Sit here. I'll be back in a minute."

When she returned with the serving tray, Claudio's cassock lay over a side chair, and he was studying the pages she'd drawn.

"You should have asked first," she said, "though you're welcome to see everything."

A guilty look flashed across his face. "It seems you have found new inspiration."

"I've only drawn Sean from memory, so things aren't perfect in his sketches. He's taking supper here tonight. I might ask him to pose."

"I am certain he will not deny your request."

She laughed. "Does that mean he doesn't love me as much as you do? Only true love will deny that which is not good for the other person."

Claudio looked toward the doorway and lowered his voice. "I try to do what is right."

"And you're successful, Deacon De Fiore." She poured him a cup of tea and smiled reassuringly.

"Should we not wait for—"

"Alex was called into the city, and I'd forgotten that my parents had plans in Point Clear today."

He raised his eyebrows skeptically and set his cup on the table. "Then I should go."

"No, please, Claudio. It's been difficult for me. I need someone who will help me feel whole."

He touched her knee. "You have gone through much with your family, but I cannot stay with you like this."

"But you must help me eat. Rosemary will get in trouble for feeding me such rich foods. We're entertaining tonight and dining at the hotel on Saturday. You know how Mother is." Eliza's hands went to her middle. "She thinks me too fat to find a suitor."

His hand cupped her cheek. "You are gorgeous the way you are."

Arms about him, Eliza snuggled into Claudio's warm neck. "I really like Sean," she whispered. "We've been talking and playing off each other all year, but yesterday showed me how wonderful he truly is."

"The two of you are good for each other."

"Well suited in our debauched ways, you mean." Her laugh fell into a small sob, and she nuzzled under his jaw. "Oh, Claudio. How am I to continue when my parents push for the match?" He rubbed her back and she shifted closer, seeking comfort.

"Will that not be a blessing?" he asked.

"Everything they push me to ends badly because it is all about them. I cannot knowingly please them because I will lose a part of myself."

"Not if you have Sean."

"Do you truly think so?"

"You must have hope, Eliza." He kissed her forehead. "Now let us eat so I may be on my way."

***

By the time Eliza's parents returned, Claudio was gone and the evidence of the forbidden tea had been cleaned. Eliza was forced to bathe and then be laced into a corset by her unforgiving mother. Unable to sit, she paced her room in her shimmering pink gown more fitting for a cotillion than a supper at home.

Just before seven, the carriage rolled into the yard with the whinny of horses. From one of the front windows, Eliza watched Alexander and Sean at the gate. Her brother wore a navy business suit—the jacket over his arm—and Sean a splendid tuxedo with a white bowtie. The electric rush at seeing his smile from her vantage point prickled the length of her. Wishing to see him closer, she ran for the stairs in her heeled slippers.

Certain that her mother would scold her to no end if she made anything other than a dainty entrance, Eliza slowed in the upper hall. She calmly lifted the edge of her skirt as she descended the main staircase.

Sean and Alexander were in the entryway. The visitor raised his eyes to watch Eliza's journey, clearly appreciating first her exposed ankles then the expanse of her décolletage.

"Miss Eliza, it's always a pleasure to see you." He offered his hand and kissed the back of hers, to which Eliza offered a deep bow showcasing the excellent corset work and lift to her full bosom.

"Mr. Spunner, I welcome you." She gave him a saucy wink before turning to Alexander. His glowing smile was one of a man replenished with strokes to his ego and physical love, but she saved her admonishing for later. "And dear brother, I'm happy to have you home."

"Thank you." Alexander went for the stairs to change clothes, leaving Sean to escort Eliza into the parlor.

George stood from his armchair beside the unlit hearth. "Welcome, Mr. Spunner. It's good to see you in relaxed circumstances. May I present my wife, Ruth?"

Eliza stayed by the settee while Sean approached her parents.

"It was a pleasant surprise to receive the invitation, Mr. and Mrs. Melling. I have enjoyed the company of your daughter several times at gatherings this past season and have always valued my association with Alexander." He bent over Ruth's hand. "I see where Eliza inherited her striking looks from, Mrs. Melling. Thank you for hosting me."

Ruth twittered under his praise and smoothed the pale blue of her well-fitting gown. "For the enjoyment of all involved, we must increase our time together, Mr. Spunner."

"Please call me Sean."

George motioned to the settee and offered a pre-supper drink that Sean accepted as he sat beside Eliza. Her father brought Sean a snifter of brandy and Eliza a small amount of disgusting sherry—the same as her mother drank. Sipping as she half-listened to her father drone on about some judge, Eliza studied Sean's profile. His nose could be considered large, though under his prominent brow it was well proportioned to his face. But it was Sean's smile that caused her heart to flutter when he looked at her.

Alexander entered the room with a confident air. He nodded to his father and kissed his mother's cheek, then he swooped past the settee on the way to the decanters, taking Eliza's glass. "Allow me to freshen your drink."

He returned in a moment with a dash of brandy for Eliza and twice as much for himself. Dinner was announced minutes later.

"Escort me, Alexander." Ruth took his arm. "I daresay working today gave you a healthy glow."

"It was rather stimulating, Mother."

Eliza looked at Sean with a knowing smirk.

"You must not allow the past to keep shadowing you, Alexander." Ruth lovingly touched her son's cheek. "I do wish you would have gone to visit your cousins this summer. The change of scenery would have done you well."

Supper conversation was ruled by George. He relished boasting of his connections and drawing Sean into his power play. Ready to stomp up the stairs and rip off her corset, Eliza reluctantly took Alexander's offered arm to escort her from the table afterward.

"I think I need to retire," Ruth said as they all entered the parlor. "It was a long day and the heat was tiresome."

"I'll be happy to see you to your room and leave the post-supper entertainment to the younger generation," George said. "Thank you for coming, Sean. We'll see you at the hotel Saturday evening. I trust Alex to keep your glass full and Eliza to see to your every need."

Goodnights were exchanged, then Eliza, Alexander, and Sean were left in the red room sharing looks of relief and excitement. After a brief pause, Alexander hurried to the decanters and poured brandy for everyone. Sean led Eliza to the smaller settee along the back wall and tugged her beside him upon the velvet cushion.

"You look ravishing in that gown." His finger trailed her ruffled cleavage, dipping into the valley as he leaned closer to nip her ear. "I think the poet Keats said it best when he wrote:

> Pillow'd upon my fair love's ripening breast
> To feel for ever its soft fall and swell
> Awake for ever in a sweet unrest
> Still, still to hear her tender-taken breath
> And so live ever—or else swoon to death."

Longing burned through Eliza at his words and touch. She instinctively brought her lips to his, tasting with a gentled fervor.

Alexander presented their glasses before them, forcing their contact to halt. "Swooning over my sister isn't allowed on my watch."

"Forget swooning." Sean kissed her once more, ending the contact with a biting tug. "My body is pulsing for her."

"Keep your pants on." Alexander settled in the adjacent armchair with his glass.

"Why should he when you had your needs seen to today?" Eliza took a swallow and kept her eyes on her brother as he lit a cigarette. "What I'd offer is a heap better than anything found in one of those establishments."

"And save him the cash too." Alexander laughed. "Though Prudie, that sweet creature, didn't wish to take my money when she saw how sad I was. Before leaving, I had to tuck the cash into—"

"I know those women lavish you with your every desire," Eliza said, "but don't go back. They'll never give you what you *need*."

He blew a smoke ring then slugged back half his brandy. "And what's that, all-knowing sister?"

"Your heart's true love—Lucy Easton." Alexander's hands tremored, and Eliza continued. "You owe it to the both of you to try. Why not write her a let—"

Alexander jumped to his feet. "Do you not think I've written dozens and burned them all because I can never express on paper the spectrum of emotions and the depth of my pain for breaking her trust? No more, Eliza! Be happy that I gain an ounce of comfort from my visits to my old girls in this lake of misery I've been drowning in for five months."

He went out the front door, and they heard his dress shoes clipping across the porch as he continued to smoke and drink. Eliza turned away from Sean and leaned into the corner of the settee. A gentleman would have given her space, but Sean acted as a lover.

"Kitten, don't fret over Alex so much." He kissed the exposed skin below her neck. "It's not ideal that he's visiting the district, but things will settle down as his heart heals."

Seeking to quiet her emotional display, she used sarcasm. "And how much experience do you have with broken hearts and the district?"

He turned her to him and lifted her chin, eyes intense in the soft gaslight. "I have a couple years on your brother and have seen a lot. I had my heart broken at seventeen and broke several others after that to keep it from happening to me again."

"What did she do to you?"

"She died. Damn yellow fever." His Adam's apple bobbed as he swallowed his emotions. "As for the district, it was never a habit for me like it is with some of the fellows. But I swear to you, Eliza Rose Melling, I haven't gone there since we kissed at John's poker party this spring."

His earnestness flooded her senses with a hunger for devotion. Overwhelmed, Eliza tucked against him. He stroked her back and trailed a hand up her bare arm.

"I want to care for you, Eliza. And I swear to help Alex as well. You've been alone in your battles. Open those gates along with your arms and I'll be by your side forevermore."

The rush of love and wonder was heady to her inflamed state. She brought their lips together in a delicious submission.

Chapter Eleven

Claudio straightened from the flower bed he was weeding when he heard the familiar sound of Eliza riding Flora into the churchyard. He wiped his sweaty brow and turned to the glowing figure in a beige riding habit and hat.

"Good morning, Claudio." She dismounted and wasted no time coming to him for kisses.

"It is a pleasant surprise to see you since I am dining at Seacliff Cottage this evening."

It was September first, and the Mellings' summer season came to an end following Labor Day. In recognition of his growing friendship with Alexander and Eliza, Mrs. Melling had invited Claudio to dine with the family one final time that Friday evening, something he had not done since Sean Spunner had shown interest in Eliza.

"I wanted to extend an invitation," she said with a smile. When he caught her blue-violet gaze, she continued. "Alex wants you to meet him at the Daphne pier and take the ferry to Montrose with him and Sean. He's staying the weekend with us instead of at the hotel. Mother insisted."

"I see." Claudio bent to pull the last weed from the space.

"I think he means to propose soon. I want you to get to know him more and make sure you still think he's good for me."

A bittersweet smile found his lips. "Your happiness proves he is good for you, *la mia Rose*. But I will do as you wish."

"Thank you, Claudio." She flung her arms about his sweat-soaked shirt and kissed him. "I'll miss you when I return to the city next week. May I write you?"

"I would look forward to it."

They said goodbye and Claudio washed in preparation for visiting a few elderly parishioners. He took a cold luncheon with the other deacon and completed more visits before he met the ferry.

Alexander waved him onboard the boat and paid his fare. After exchanging greetings, he leaned closer to Claudio. His blue eyes were clear, and he appeared joyful.

"I need you to help me encourage Eliza to matrimony," he whispered. "Sean's serious about her, and she needs to settle down before she ends up like me. It would be a thousand times worse for her."

Claudio nodded.

"She trusts your judgment, Claudio. Advise her to move forward with Sean when he declares himself to her."

"I will do my best."

Sean stood from a bench nearby, suitcases at his feet. "Hello, Deacon De Fiore."

"I am Claudio, please. The Mellings are like family to me."

"As I hope to be soon as well." Sean's smile held honorable intentions.

The three men settled together on the bench and smoked for the remainder of the boat trip. They climbed the hill in Montrose where Mr. Campbell waited with the carriage. At Seacliff Cottage's front gate, Claudio took one of the suitcases and followed the others inside the house.

"Allow me to help, Master Melling," Leroy said in the entry hall.

"We can handle things. We're all going upstairs to get ready for supper."

Alexander led the way to the small bedroom beside his and pointed in. "I'm going to use the bath first, if you don't mind."

"By all means." Sean nodded his thanks and continued into the room.

A large cream-colored envelope waited in the middle of the blue bedspread, his name boldly inscribed across it. Sean set his suitcase on the luggage rack at the foot of the bed and picked up the correspondence. Removing a pen from his breast pocket, he ran it under the seal.

"Thank you for carrying the other case, Claudio. Mrs. Melling likes people to dress for supper, so I had to bring two monkey suits besides my day clothes. You're lucky to have a uniform that can be worn in all circumstances. But seeing as how I'd do anything to please the parents, I can't complain."

Claudio set the second suitcase on top of the first and turned to leave as Sean pulled the paper from the envelope.

"Dear Lord!" Sean whistled. "God truly blessed that girl, and I mean it sincerely, Deacon. She's perfect."

He turned the picture toward Claudio. A self-portrait of Eliza reflected within the sketched outline of a mirror's frame showcased her bare from the waist up. Tousled dark hair hung over her naked shoulders, the tips curling about firm breasts. Only her eyes—the perfect blue-violet shade as they shone in sunlight—left a touch of color amid the pencil drawing. Despite the pleasing curves of her body, Claudio found his gaze directed to those haunting eyes above her perfect lips.

"Am I not the luckiest man alive?" Sean unintentionally gloated.

"*Sí*, Eliza is wonderful. I will see you downstairs."

Before Claudio reached the parlor, Eliza caught him at the foot of the stairs.

"I saw you go with Sean to his room," she whispered. "Did he find the envelope?"

Thinking of the vision that lay beneath Eliza's fine purple gown had his throat dry, but Claudio nodded.

"Did he like it?"

"Of course he liked it," he said in an angry whisper. "But it was not a righteous thing to do."

She gave him a wicked smile. "I've never claimed to be a saint."

***

Eliza flounced into the parlor before Claudio could admonish her sinfulness any further. She found no shame in the sketch since Sean had practically seen all she had to offer when they'd gone swimming in the Gulf two months earlier.

The deacon is jealous because he wishes to have me for himself.

"Eliza, please act with decorum," her mother said. "Offer Deacon De Fiore a drink."

He came into the room behind her, face solemn as he greeted her parents, who were sitting in their chairs before the hearth like royalty on thrones.

"What may I fix for you, Claudio?" Eliza asked when he sat on the end of the settee.

"Nothing, thank you." He fingered his crucifix, looking like a sulking boy.

Eliza took the scrolled armchair beside the settee so that she faced the doorway but could look upon Claudio at the same time. Her mother prattled on for the better part of half an hour about the coming social events in Mobile. When Alexander and Sean appeared, Eliza couldn't help the smile that formed. Sean was quick to cross the room while his eyes roamed her body. He leaned in for a kiss on the cheek as he held her hands.

"Thank you for the welcome gift." In a louder voice he added, "You look beautiful, Eliza."

He moved along to greet her mother, and Alexander delivered a glass of wine to Eliza before he took the spot beside Claudio with a snifter of brandy.

Eliza pursed her lips. "Aren't you going to offer—"

"No," Alexander said with a smile.

"Mr. Melling, might I take a private word with you?" Sean asked.

"Anytime, my boy." George stood and clapped him on the shoulder. "Come to my den."

Seeing him with her father set a cold fear in Eliza's stomach. *What will Father make him promise if he asks permission to propose to me? What dealings will be done to secure my hand?* The door to the back room closed with an echo down the hall.

"Eliza," Ruth said, "I am sure it will be an emotional boost to secure a proposal of marriage during your first year in society, but do not feel you need to accept it." She fluffed the sleeves of her navy gown. "He's handsome enough and on solid financial footing for twenty-five, but you could do much better than an orphan raised by his uncle's charity."

"She's happy, Mother," Alexander said. "That's the only thing that matters."

She glared at her son. "You cannot live off happiness."

"But it's no life without it." He slung back the remainder of his drink and stood to refill the glass.

A wave of sadness over Alexander's lost joy caused Eliza to bite her lip to keep it from trembling, and Claudio caught her gaze.

"Follow your heart," he whispered. "It will not lead you astray."

She crossed her arms, hands gripping the opposite limbs in a pathetic replacement for a hug she desperately needed.

When her father and Sean returned, Alexander immediately brought his friend to the decanters, but George Melling towered over the space—eyes settling on his daughter.

"You look chilled, Eliza. Go fetch one of your pretty wraps."

She hurried to her room before her mother could protest that it would crush the organza flowers on her plunging neckline. Taking a pewter lace shawl from a drawer, Eliza brought it around her shoulders. The mirror reflected the nervousness on her pale complexion, and she cursed her parents under her breath for turning what should be a wonderful day into another night of oppression under their rule. Looking at the sketch of Sean she had tucked into the corner of her mirror, she immediately smiled over his joyful countenance she'd captured in the drawing.

I will be happy with him. Gloriously happy.

Her lightened steps came to a halt at the top of the main stairs. Her father stood at the bottom, the black of his tuxedo a stain on the red carpet beneath his feet. He gripped her arm to stop her before she could pass.

"You will marry him, Eliza. Sean will join Melling and Associates, and I'll be sure he provides you with everything you need in life, just as I have done for you since you were born."

She shivered, and his grip slackened.

"You have a chill, just as I said." He walked her into the parlor. "Alex, your sister needs a bit of brandy to warm her. There, girl, settle between the men and you'll be warm in no time."

Eliza obediently took the center position on the settee between Claudio and Sean. The latter took her hand into his and pressed his lips to her knuckles before resting their clasped hands on his thigh. On her other side, Claudio's calming presence held her to sanity like a fire amid the chilled atmosphere her father controlled.

A moment later, Alexander pressed the shot of brandy into her left hand before claiming a chair for himself. Eliza wanted to sling it back, but she took dainty sips under her mother's glare.

George spoke of the brunch they had attended that morning, all the important people he had spoken with and who owed him favors. To his credit, Sean did his best to follow the predominantly one-sided conversation and remarked when polite, but none of the others seemed to have an ounce of concern for the topic.

Relief washed over Eliza when Leroy announced supper. George offered his arm to his wife and motioned Claudio and Alexander from the room before them.

"At last, a moment alone." Sean pulled Eliza into his arms, set her lace shawl on the settee, and nipped her unadorned neck. "You look amazing."

He kissed her firmly on the mouth then across her collarbone. Lowering his attentions to the swell of her chest, he tongued her cleavage until she gasped. Chuckling, he straightened and the gleam in his eyes melted her fears.

"Your lovely drawing has me wanting to taste every inch of you." He started for the door with her hand respectfully around his arm. "Having you back in the city will be terrific. Parties, shows—I'll invite you out as often as possible."

Eliza smiled throughout supper, although her clothing didn't allow much room to eat. Halfway through the main course, Sean leaned closer to her, his dark brows knitted together.

"Are you not hungry?"

Heart in her throat, she nearly wept for his perceptiveness. He'd been with her when she was *inappropriately* attired—according to her mother's standards—and therefore free to eat however she liked without the constraints of a corset.

"I'm too excited to eat," she lied.

His hand trailed her knee and he whispered, "Soon, Kitten."

After supper, Alexander stood first. "I propose a walk to help settle this fine meal."

"It's much too late, Alex," his mother said. "And Claudio must leave."

"We can say our goodbyes to Claudio on the way out." Alexander took the last swallow of wine from his fluted glass and looked at his father.

"Let them go, Ruth. Alexander will chaperone, and we can retire whenever you wish."

"If you insist." She sighed then turned to Claudio. "I appreciate your kindness to us this summer, Deacon De Fiore. We shall see you once more at Mass, but do take care of yourself. I hope you will visit when we return."

Claudio kissed her cheeks then shook all the men's hands before Eliza claimed his arm. Leroy was sent to give word to Mr. Campbell to ready the carriage, and Eliza walked the deacon to the front porch. He breathed deeply of the night air, seeming to relax in the darkness.

"Will all be well for me, Claudio?"

He turned to her. "*Sí, la mia Rose.* You will do well. Sean cares for you, and I believe his passion will satisfy your needs."

"I hope so, because my passion unfulfilled tends to get me into trouble."

"I will see you on the Sabbath." He lovingly traced a cross on her forehead and kissed her cheeks in farewell.

Eliza watched the carriage pull away as Alexander and Sean joined her on the porch.

"Shall you thank me now or later, Eliza Rose?" Alexander flashed his impish smile as he turned up a low-burning oil lantern.

"Now *and* later, I suspect." She kissed his cheek then attached herself to Sean's arm. "Lead the way, brother."

He brought them into the forest along the path she often traveled to her favorite rock. But rather than going to the cliff, he stopped in a tiny meadow rimmed with ferns. After setting the lantern on the ground, he made a swirling motion with his finger. Understanding his meaning, Eliza immediately stood in front of him and turned around.

"Spunner, I officially pass this duty on to you." Alexander began opening the fasteners on the back of Eliza's gown.

"What—" Sean began.

"Ruth Melling might look genteel but she's cruel when it comes to women's fashion. My sister suffers horribly under our mother." Back of the gown open, Alexander deftly loosened her corset laces without looking. "As soon as she's away from Mother, you must relieve Eliza from her confinement."

Sean stared open-mouthed as Eliza's gown drooped lower in the front. The jiggling of her breasts under Alexander's ministrations held him so captivated that Eliza had to laugh.

"And now you know one of our family secrets." She raised an innocent brow. "My figure isn't nearly as firm as people believe."

"No," Sean said with a grin. "It's better. Your sketch and the time in the Gulf with you proved that."

Alexander laughed as he loosely retied the corset then nudged her toward Sean. "I'll leave it to you to get her dress properly closed in the back. And here—she's usually ravenous." He pulled a dinner roll from his tuxedo jacket and shoved it at Sean before dropping to the forest floor with a bottle of brandy he removed from another pocket.

Sean laughed and passed the roll to Eliza, who ate it without pause. "I always said the Melling siblings were the most fun, but I can't say I'm in a hurry to refasten your gown."

"I'd be disappointed if you were." Eliza pulled the trailing gown up in one arm and took his hand in her other. "Come with me."

"Are you going to seduce me with your brother right here?"

"We both know I wouldn't have to work at seduction." She brought him to the cliff. "But Alex never goes farther than that spot in the forest. Here's another family secret—he's afraid of heights."

"What?"

She nodded. "No haylofts, no cliffs. When I heard about the Dardenne Masquerade last year—how Eddie had to carry him out the third floor window and down the fire escape—I knew in an instant he didn't pass out from drugs or drinking. It was fear, plain and simple."

"So the mighty Alexander has more paralyzing enemies than losing Lucy?"

"Yes, but don't tell anyone."

"I aim to protect and love you, and that includes helping Alex." He trailed his hands over the curve of her shoulders, further dropping the gown's front. "And I'm pleased to learn part of that duty includes undressing you."

Beneath the sparkling stars over the bay, their kisses deepened. Eliza paused long enough to step out of her gown. She hung it over a tree limb, taking a moment to study the way the purple fabric shimmered in the moonlight when the breeze rustled it. Sean followed her lead and left his tuxedo jacket on an adjacent branch. He took her onto his knee as he settled on her special rock, using the lift of her breasts the corset provided to feast upon her.

"Do you still glory in my tits, Sean Spunner?"

"I hope to lavish them all the days of my life, Kitten." He suckled a passion mark above the ruffle concealing her peaks before hugging her to him. "I didn't expect to ask you in such a compromising position, but there's a ring in my jacket pocket. Marry me, Eliza Rose Melling. Marry me, and we'll share this passion for years to come."

"I never thought I'd feel love like this," she said. "Every inch of me wants to feel you against me, to know everything about you, inside and out."

He claimed her mouth as he cupped a breast with one hand and locked his fingers in her hair with his other. Allowing their passion to guide them, they touched and explored. Eliza knew he wouldn't go all the way in their present location—not for their first time together—and lowered her guard to enjoy the sensation of being in Sean's secure arms.

After a while, she laid her cheek on the soft fabric of his shirt and curled into his lap.

"You feel so good," he said as he smoothed her hair.

"My room is the attic. Join me if you wish."

Sean laughed. "As much as I'd love to, Kitten, I won't disrespect your parents by taking you under their roof."

"It's going to be a long three nights."

"You can be patient."

"Patience doesn't run in my family."

"Speaking of, we'd better get Alex back to the house, shouldn't we? I'm not sure how full that bottle was that he brought."

Eliza squeezed him in a hug and rewarded him with a kiss. "Thank you for loving me and caring for my brother."

"He's been my brother too these past few years. A Mystics of Dardenne member is always a brother." Sean helped her into her gown and fastened it closed. Then he dropped to his knee before her with the ring—his lopsided smile and chipped tooth making him look boyish under the moonlight, though he was over seven years her senior. "To make it official. Eliza Rose Melling, will you be my wife?"

"Yes!"

Sean slipped the gold band with a sizeable diamond solitaire onto her ring finger then claimed another deep kiss. Arm in arm, she led him back to Alexander. Her brother sat at the base of a large oak, eyes closed and the bottle clutched to his chest.

"Come on, Melling." Sean released Eliza and hauled Alexander to his feet by his armpits.

"Is your relationship consummated already?"

"No, but she's wearing my ring."

Blood-shot eyes wide, Alexander lurched for Eliza. "Congratulations! Now don't wait too long for the wedding. The gossips will say what they want. Don't deny your pleasures to meet their demands. They'll find something to chatter about anyway."

***

Despite the late night, Eliza woke with the sun on Saturday. She pulled her dressing gown over a short summer nightie, grabbed her sketchbook, and stealthily descended the attic stairs. She slipped into the unlocked door to the guest room and took in everything about the way Sean lived. A suitcase was open on the rack with a pile of underthings jumbled inside, and another piece of luggage stood on the floor beside it. In the open wardrobe, his tuxedos and suits hung in a neat row, shoes on the bottom ledge.

Sean was tangled in his sheets wearing only his underdrawers, head half off a pillow and a bare foot sticking out from the bottom of the blankets. He looked like a romance hero after a pleasurable night, and Eliza hoped impassioned dreams about her had something to do with it.

She silently perched on the armchair near the window. The drapes allowed in enough light for her to study his softened features and capture them on paper. She drew his face first, including the morning stubble shadowing his jaw in a sign of virility. Thick brows over his closed eyes and his tousled hair were next. His shoulders—why had Edmund's captivated her when Sean was clearly better built—made her heart quicken. To get his chest and abdomen just right, she wanted to run her hands and tongue over him.

Curse that arrogant Easton chin and stupid broad shoulders! I could have been enjoying Sean from the beginning of the year if I hadn't been blinded by Eddie's smooth ways.

The manly torso she sketched blended into the lines of the sheets. Dark chest hair and shadowed valleys of his muscles brought life to the silent figure on the page. The urge to climb into the bed with him to ease the burden of the shame that now rolled across her soul increased. Instead, she tucked her pencil behind her ear and slumped against the back of the chair.

Tears cascaded her cheeks as she continued to watch the man she loved as he slumbered peacefully. She hugged the sketchbook to her chest and bit her lip to keep her crying from turning to sobs. Her father's footsteps went down the hall to the stairs, but still she held vigil.

It was another half hour before Sean stirred. Eliza watched in fascination as he stretched and scratched to alertness with a series of small groans that endeared him to her even more. He sat up and rubbed his eyes, glancing around the room as he did so. When he turned toward the chair, he jerked.

"God, you scared me, Eliza! What—how long have you been here?"

"About an hour." She clutched the book to her heart.

Focusing on her face, Sean seemed to register the dried tears. He fell to his knees before her.

"What is it?" He took her hands into one of his, kissing the ring. "You haven't changed your mind, have you?"

Eliza shook her head, and he smoothed her unbound hair. "I'm sorry," she whispered.

"For what? Did you peek under the blankets while I was snoring?" He glanced to his scarcely covered groin. "I'd like to think it's nothing to be sorry about, but one never knows what a girl has in mind these days."

Her laughter was loud, and he covered her mouth with his hand.

"So you're sorry for bringing the household's attention to the fact that you and I are in my bedroom first thing in the morning wearing next to nothing?" His other hand went to her knee within the opened robe and caressed her skin in tiny circles. The fingers over her mouth followed the line of her jaw. He dropped the sketchbook into her lap so he could trace the curves of her chest. "Kitten, you'll be the death of me looking as you do in your nightclothes, with this vulnerability I've never seen. Tell me how I can help you so I can bring you somewhere that won't get us in trouble if we're caught by your parents."

"I'm sorry about Edmund—what I did with him that night. I want my body to be only for you."

He cupped her face in his palms. The sun coming stronger through the windows gave his eyes the amber light she craved. "That's the sweetest, most generous declaration I've ever heard, though apologies aren't necessary. We were nothing but acquaintances back then."

"Then you——"

Sean's lips went to hers. His mouth was dry from sleep, but she soaked in his devotion nevertheless. After a minute, he nudged her back in the chair and tucked her wayward robe around her body.

"Some of the fellows warned me you were a shallow flirt, but I could sense the depth in your soul. Don't doubt your worthiness, especially to me. But don't expect me to list names and infractions to my fiancée. Confession to a priest is enough, don't you agree?"

"I don't know," she stated honestly. "I haven't confessed that sin. I never felt guilty about it until now."

Sean crushed her to his chest. "You truly love me," he said with relief as though part of him doubted it. Then he lifted the sketchbook. "Are you gifting me another drawing?"

"I worked on something for myself." She opened to the new sketch. "You're as captivating in sleep as you are awake."

"Your naughty side is perfection, Kitten. Are you going to look at this while you lie in bed?"

"Is that what you did last night with your sketch? You look like you had a night of passionate dreams at the very least." She leaned the book against the chair leg and moved onto Sean's lap.

He took her hips and shifted her closer, eyes darkening as his arousal was made known. "I looked upon your succulent image until I was nearly blind."

She wanted to ask if his arm was tired too, but his mischievous glint answered that suspicion. Gently rocking atop him, she grinned. "Maybe I'll do the same with this sketch tonight. Unless I can claim the real thing."

"You debauched angel." He buried his face in her décolletage, sucking kisses until he came up for air. "I'm not making love to you in your parents' house while I'm a guest."

"There's the cliffs, the stables, the beach."

He hauled her to her feet and spanked her. "Go, you little minx, before I take you right now and ruin our prospects of a blessed union."

She took his admonishment as a declaration of love and happily retreated to prepare for the day. When she entered the dining room an hour later, a powder-blue tea gown draped her uncorseted body in lace. Sean stood from his seat and pulled out her chair, twinkling eyes and grin putting her at ease although her parents watched from the head and foot of the table. They had been in bed when Eliza, Sean, and Alexander returned from their "walk" the previous night, but they clearly knew what had happened in regard to the proposal.

Ruth held out her hand before Eliza could pass around the table. "Allow me to see it so I may judge how much Mr. Spunner loves you."

"There's not a diamond large enough in the world to showcase my feelings for your daughter, Mrs. Melling." Sean kept his tone respectable, though he appeared nervous over his future mother-in-law's judgment.

Eliza unflinchingly placed her left hand in her mother's. "Sean captured my style perfectly."

Ruth sniffed and lifted her chin toward Sean. "It will do, though keep a larger stone in mind after she produces a firstborn son."

"Thank you, Mrs. Melling." The words were said automatically, for Sean's attention was completely on Eliza as she came to his side. He was bold enough to put his arms about her and kiss her on the lips. "Good morning, Eliza. I hope you slept well."

"I did, thank you." Sean pushed in her chair after she sat then he returned to his, linking their hands under the table.

Rosemary came in with coffee, eggs, and toast and set about serving everyone. When she reached Eliza, Ruth cleared her throat. The cook left a half portion on Eliza's plate.

"Excuse me, Miss Rosemary," Sean said. "It smells wonderful. Could I please have a bit more?"

"Yes, sir."

As soon as Rosemary left, Sean slid a third of his food onto Eliza's dish.

Ruth gasped.

"I don't mean to be impertinent, Mrs. Melling, but Eliza's wellbeing is my prime concern. Her art and horsemanship require a lot of energy, and hearty meals are important to provide that. I don't aim for my bride to grow faint because she skimped at meals in a vain attempt to meet some standard of beauty. If I may speak freely—and I don't do so to be vulgar—your daughter's form is excessively attractive. From her beautiful, come-hither eyes to her hips that are the perfect—"

George roared with laughter. Ruth turned red with indignation, but Eliza's love swelled within until she thought she'd burst.

"Mr. Spunner, I have never—"

"Come now, Ruth," George said. "I want my daughter to have a husband who is man enough to take control of a situation. Anyone who risks his standing with his future mother-in-law has what it takes. Welcome to the family, Sean."

"Not too soon," Ruth snapped. "There is to be no wedding until next summer. Eliza is, after all, only eighteen and—"

"I'm nineteen in two months, Mother. You were the same age when you married."

"There's nothing tackier than holiday weddings, and I refuse to host one during carnival season or Lent."

Eliza huffed her annoyance. "We can do something within the next two months. Alex advised—"

"Taking wedding advice from someone who has not successfully accomplished one is asinine."

George changed the subject to gain control. "I'll leave the wedding planning to the women, Sean, but I'd like to make an appointment with you in the near future to discuss bringing you into Melling and Associates."

"Thank you for your confidence, Mr. Melling. I'd be happy to meet with you."

They shook hands while Eliza watched with dread.

AUTUMN

Chapter Twelve

Claudio held the floral embossed letter under his nose, breathing in the rose scent before reading. It was the second letter that week—the fifth for the month. He'd tried to help Eliza from across the bay, but her letters were increasingly agitated. Sighing, he settled on his bed and read.

> *September 26, 1905*
> *Dearest Claudio,*
> *I do not know what I am to do with myself with both Alexander and Father pushing me toward Sean. I begged Sean not to join the firm until after Christmas. Fortunately, he agreed. Since Mother is refusing a wedding until spring, it would make no difference if he's in the family business this year or next. But Father is eager to control Sean's career—for my own benefit he tells me.*
> *Sean takes Sunday dinner with us after late Mass each week, but I cannot enjoy the time with my parents presiding. This Sunday was blessedly different. As you know, my parents spent the weekend at Seacliff—Mother said she saw you in Daphne when they went for a carriage ride—so Alex chaperoned the meal. The three of us ate and drank too much then Sean and I spent a glorious few hours in the camellia maze while Alex slept off his indulgences. And before you*

ask—though I know you never would—Sean and I have not consummated our relationship, though we have shared many pleasures.

I have insisted on coming to Seacliff next month. Alex and I will be on the ferry Friday, October 13. If you would like to dine with us that evening, send word and you can join us when we dock at Daphne. Otherwise—or additionally—see if you can join us for an afternoon ride and picnic that Saturday. Spending time with you is always grounding, and I need to reestablish my priorities.

Mother thinks all my time should be spent in preparation for the Halloween Flirts dance. She believes it is an honor that I was asked to participate in preparing for this secret society dance when I am not yet pledged to one of the mystic groups. I think the women just wanted use of my art skills since I am in charge of painting backdrops and scenery for them to create a "Haunted Graveyard" themed dance. Since The Church of the Assumption is more quaint compared to what we have in Mobile, I am using it as the model for the main canvas that will fill the wall behind the dais. When I am done with that canvas, I will work on smaller ones depicting headstones and trees under the night sky. There is no challenge in this project, but I must complete it. Even Father urges me to do so as it will give my art a large audience from the affluent families in town, though the revelers will be too drunk to appreciate it.

I work all day in my studio on the Halloween project. Mother drops in to check on me and Father inspects it several times a week when he returns from work. Alex, too. He stops by to share a smoke with me before we dress for supper if he's taking it at home. Sean dines with him at Aethelwulf Club once a week, but I do believe my brother is still going to the district, though he's stopped telling me. He did attend confession when

Claudio requested the time off from Father Angelo. With the Saturday secured, he settled at his plain writing desk to compose his return letter. Hoping to remind Eliza of their carefree summer, he wrote of the blessing of the jubilee they had enjoyed the month before. Spending the night on the bay with her, Alexander, and the Watts family as they'd gathered the seafood harvest that washed onto the shores was one of his favorite memories. Eliza had shined like a daughter of the night with her dark hair and laughing eyes as she'd filled her bucket and further occupied Claudio's heart.

For the next two and a half weeks, Claudio worked and worshiped. Several evenings a week were spent replying to Eliza's frequent letters. He found an empty cookie box in the kitchen that he claimed as a souvenir in which to collect her correspondences. The red-and-blue tin turned his desk into a bright spot he looked forward to sitting at as he composed his messages of hope to long-suffering Eliza.

* * *

Mr. Campbell arrived to collect him at noon on October fourteenth. Claudio spent the jostling carriage ride in contemplation and prayer, hoping to erect his defenses against Eliza's beguiling ways.

When they arrived at Seacliff Cottage, she stood on the front porch in a simple button-front dress, legs and feet bare.

"Claudio!" She ran to him, meeting halfway across the yard with a hug that took his breath away.

"*La mia Rose.*" He pulled back after a moment and kissed her cheeks. "You look well."

She gleefully spun like a child, arms outstretched and her loose hair rising like her skirt in a twirling mass of beauty. "I'm without parents! Without constraints! Without care!" She took Claudio's hand, running for the house with him. "Leave your cassock inside today rather than the stable. I'll help."

They stopped in the hall, leaving the front door open.

"He's here, Alex!" she shouted before going at Claudio's buttons. More quietly, she added, "And he's as handsome as ever."

"Eliza," Claudio admonished.

"It's true." She kissed the corner of his mouth then lowered to her knees to continue opening his cassock.

A moment later, a figure rounded the side of the house and stepped onto the porch. Expecting to see Alexander, Claudio's surprise at meeting Sean's gaze translated to embarrassment over his position with Eliza.

"You thought you were rid of me a few days, then I find you on your knees before another man." Sean's tone was serious, but the smile on his face showed a different emotion. *Lust.*

Eliza jumped into Sean's arms with a squeal.

"Seeing you like that from a different vantage point is exciting," Sean told her as he nuzzled her neck. "But, deacon or not, I'd rather you not get in the habit of undressing another man."

She murmured something that sounded to Claudio like "you're the only one" before they were kissing each other so deeply that he had to look away. The couple stumbled blindly for the settee, bumping into the parlor's doorframe on the way.

Alexander pattered down the stairs in his riding outfit. Pausing beside Claudio, he greeted his friend then looked at Sean moving atop Eliza.

"He told me yesterday he'd take the ferry to Fairhope this morning and rent a horse, but he wanted to surprise Eliza. Was she pleased?"

Claudio frowned and turned to the front door. Alexander caught his arm and walked onto the porch with him.

"They swear they haven't had sex," Alexander whispered. "But I'm beginning to think they might as well count it as such even if it hasn't been traditional intercourse."

"There is nothing traditional about your sister."

Alexander laughed. "I think they have a bet between themselves about who can hold out the longest. They're both gamblers and hate to lose. It's making for an interesting engagement."

A quarter of an hour later, the three horses were saddled with their supplies. Claudio mounted Flora and watched Sean bring Eliza behind him. The knife struck—the pain of losing Eliza's company when he'd looked forward for weeks to riding with her arms about him. Instead he was forced to watch her hands snake down Sean's front to his groin.

"Eliza!" Sean yelped, causing their horse to jerk. "I don't wish to be manhandled in a saddle. At least not with your brother and a deacon looking on."

They laughed and her hands settled respectfully around his waist before they trotted for the path. Claudio crossed himself and nudged Flora to follow.

I cannot be sad when I prayed for protection against the pull of my attraction to her. God saved me by sending her fiancé.

Over three months had passed since he'd accompanied the group on Independence Day. There was no denying the closeness Eliza and Sean shared, but after reading the letters with her apprehensions over their engagement, Claudio could not be happy for her. She was troubled and that concerned him, even when the couple continually laughed and touched.

They took their picnic at Weeks Bay in the same place Claudio had the first time he'd ridden with the Mellings. After eating, Sean and Eliza went for a walk toward the swamp. Concerned over the wildlife since it wasn't cold like it had been during their trip at the beginning of spring, Claudio stood to go find them after half an hour of their absence.

"Sit back down," Alexander commanded. He tossed his cigarette case to Claudio.

"But there are *alligatores* with snapping jaws."

Alexander puffed out smoke with a hearty laugh. "The only jaws I'd be worried about are Sean's. He's got to be stuffing his mouth with something, and I don't want you walking in on it."

Claudio's face heated, and he lit a cigarette to give himself something to concentrate on.

"You need to get over her." Alexander's tone softened. "I know that sounds ridiculous coming from me, but you never had with Eliza what Lucy and I shared. It should be easier for you."

"God sees fit to allow me to suffer alongside her."

"She's not suffering, Claudio. I bet the swamp's been ringing with squeals of delight this hour." He ran a hand through his pale hair. "And my Lucy might be closer than ever to Frederick, but I'm going to the Halloween dance to find out. Eliza helped with the invitations, and she slipped a second one in with Freddy's, knowing he'd try to persuade Lucy to come. It would be perfect for her—a chance to get out while staying anonymous under a costume."

"Then how will you know her?"

"She could never hide from me. I know every inch of her by heart."

They sat in silence after Alexander's tragic declaration.

Eliza and Sean emerged from their exploration, she on his back with his arms under her bare knees. She slipped to the sand when they were a few feet away and took Claudio's arm. "I need to ride with you on the way back once we get to Fairhope."

He glanced at Sean who was conversing with Alexander. "Does Sean need to leave so soon?"

"He has to return Bruiser to the stable," Eliza said. "I'll send Mr. Campbell to collect Sean from town. He's going to stay the night at Seacliff." She bit her lip and looked at Claudio with shining eyes the color of the summer hydrangeas.

"But your parents are not—"

"Exactly!" She giggled. "Mother is being ridiculous by making us wait so long for our wedding. We want to share a bed for the night, but not the way you're thinking. He'll hold me, Claudio. Maybe nibble my ear to make me shiver."

She touched his ear as she said it, and Claudio's body was washed in pleasure.

"But you and I will have the ride to Seacliff for talking, and also the time until he comes back. I've missed you these weeks. Thank you for being such a great correspondent."

Before he could reset his guard, he smiled. "Your letters are wonderful, *la mia Rose*."

She planted a kiss on his cheek as she hugged him. Then Sean snatched her waist and swung her about until she shrieked with laughter.

Eliza's half-opened dress billowed behind her as they took the lead on Bruiser. Claudio kept Flora's pace slower to save her energy for when she would carry two, but Alexander let Janus loose. The horse pounded the beach as he overtook the others on the northward race.

At Fairhope, Eliza leaned against a pier column, arms crossed and a fake scowl on her pretty face. "It took you long enough. I sent

Alex home to hasten Sean's transportation." She swung up behind Claudio and tucked against him with her sensual warmth. "I know for a fact Flora is capable of much more than you're allowing her."

"*Sí*, but why hurry when our time is limited?"

She kissed him. "You miss me."

"I do. And I am concerned for your well-being. Your letters bare the heartaches you suffer because of your family."

"And you comfort me, Claudio. Knowing you care helps me survive another day."

He laid his hand atop hers on his middle. "I will never forsake you, Eliza."

"No matter what I do?"

He brought one of her hands to his heart. "You are always here, *la mia Rose*. I will help you as long as I live."

Chapter Thirteen

The evening of the Halloween Flirts dance, Eliza paced her bedroom in her mother-approved costume. The royal blue Regency gown, complete with a daringly low scooped bodice above the empire waist, was trimmed in gold braiding, which matched the decorative pins in her upswept hair. Below the cap sleeves were the longest pair of gloves she'd ever worn. Their gold expanse reached inches above her elbow. Her mother had coordinated with the seamstress for a complementary suit for Sean, but Eliza had yet to see it.

Alexander stopped in her open doorway. He wore the tight-fitting Mystics of Dardenne skeleton suit from the '04 masquerade that showcased his slim build to the best advantage, mask still in hand.

"Ready, Eliza?"

She nodded and descended the grand staircase on his arm. Their parents waited in the foyer for Eliza to pass inspection.

Ruth set upon her puffed sleeves. "Do not make a pig of yourself, Eliza. That fiancé of yours spoils you too much, and you need to set limits. Two glasses of champagne and no more than half a plate of food should be plenty."

"Leave her be, Ruth," George said. "The only thing she needs to be concerned about is people knowing who painted the scenery."

The Mellings' driver pulled the Lyman limousine to the end of the veranda, and the siblings got in the back. When they stopped at Sean's newly acquired federal style home, the driver rang the bell to collect him. Eliza's heart quickened when Sean stepped under the electric porchlight. Royal blue shawl-collared waistcoat over a gold damask vest with a smart cravat knotted nobly at his throat. His stockings and breeches accented his athletic build, and the top hat completed the extravagant ensemble.

"Control yourself, Eliza," Alexander warned. "I don't wish to be privy to your sexual play on the drive."

"Then you may wish to ride in the front because that delicious sight needs to be unwrapped."

The door opened. Sean removed his hat and leaned over to step in. His eyes fixated on Eliza as he joined her on the leather seat.

"Your mother must not hate me since she chose that gown," he said while staring at Eliza's chest. His face was unshaven, and it served to make him look like a top-notch rake of the Regency era. "Your glorious tits! They're on display like giant pearls on a shelf, ripe for harvesting. Whatever shapewear has them lifted so proudly needs a standing ovation. They're so perky I bet they could walk into the party by themselves."

Eliza's head fell against the high seatback as she laughed. Sean took the opportunity to bury his face in her cleavage. His attentions had her ready for more, but then he groaned and turned his head sideways to rest upon her like a pillow.

"These beauties are so plump I would happily suffocate down here."

Eliza smiled and kissed the top of his head. "I'm all for sharing my treats with you. Happy Halloween, Sean."

He raised his mouth to hers and they kissed until Alexander nudged them.

"We're nearly there." Alexander pulled on his mask. It was originally a full-face covering but he'd cut it so it ended at his nose in the front. His lips were practically twitching with excitement.

"Alex," Eliza said as she leaned against Sean, "please don't do anything rash. If Lucy is here, you need to go slow."

"Patience has never been my strength."

Since the Battle House hotel was being rebuilt following the February fire, the Halloween dance was being held at Temperance Hall. They waited several minutes until the carriages in front of them moved away, then the automobile pulled before the front doors. Sean exited first, donning his hat then holding out his arm to Eliza. She felt as she had beside Lucy when they'd emerged from the carriage the night of the Mystics of Dardenne masquerade in January—on top of the world. All eyes were upon Sean and her in their splendid Regency apparel.

Seeing their glowing reflection in the gilt mirrors of the lobby made Eliza catch her breath at their perfection. She paused and turned to Sean, her gloved hand on his cheek as she smiled as though the sun radiated from her soul.

"I love you, Sean. I love you and I love us together."

Their kiss caused several nearby ladies to gasp in shock, but Sean took her face in his hands and brought his lips to hers once more. Cheek to cheek, he whispered, "I love you too."

Eliza vaguely registered Alexander behind them as they entered the ballroom. Taking in the sight of her art around the room, a shiver ran through her body. Never had she worked on such a large scale. The looming silhouette of the wooden structure of Church of the Assumption was captured over ten feet high on the giant canvas against the backdrop of an eerie night sky of midnight blue. The smaller panels complemented the potted trees and faux tombstones placed about the room, giving it a surreal effect within the dimmed lights.

"It's wonderful, Eliza!" Sean grabbed the next man who walked by. "Do you see all this, Leonard? My fiancée painted it. She's as talented as she is gorgeous, wouldn't you agree?"

On and on Sean gushed about the murals, stopping only long enough to acquire drinks for them. Eliza continued to smile and nod at the people Sean wrangled into a conversation, but her eyes began to roam the room as it filled with revelers.

Frederick, in black swashbuckler threads complete with a highwayman-style mask that covered his hair and upper face, stood near the corner across the way. Eliza knew it was him by the girth of his thighs in the slim-fitting pants and the span of his shoulders beneath his short cape. Utterly dashing! When he stepped to the side, he revealed Lucy in traditional Victorian mourning garb—something straight out of the Eastons' attic. She sat erect, black-gloved hands clasped on her lap, twisting a handkerchief. The black lace veil hid her features in the shadowed room, but another noticed her as well. When Frederick went for refreshments, Alexander approached her from the opposite side.

"Quick!" Eliza grabbed Sean's arm as he was in the middle of a conversation with a man dressed as Count Dracula. "Go speak with

Frederick while he collects food. Talk to him about boxing—anything! Just keep him busy as long as possible!"

She skimmed along the edge of the crowd, hoping to get close enough without interfering to hear what transpired between the former lovers. She moved behind a ficus less than ten feet to Lucy's left.

Alexander stopped a few steps before Lucy and bowed low in a humble gesture. "It saddens this mass of bones to see a fine lady mourning the loss of a loved one."

"It's been more than eight months since I lost my first love," Lucy's voice trembled.

Alexander took a step forward. "He would take all the pain from you if he could."

Lucy's breath caught, but she shook her head. "Taking the pain would erase all the good. I never wish to part with those memories."

Alexander grew bold with her confession, dropping to a knee before her. "And I, Lucy. Our love was magnificent and could be so again."

The handkerchief went under her veil, and she shook her head once more.

"I'm doing better," Alexander continued, "but I'd progress more with you by my side, my queen. I've been in agony these months, but if you're happy, I'll be happy for you." He took the hand on her lap into his own black-gloved one. "Tell me you love Freddy like you loved me and I'll walk away. Tell me your passion for him is as bright or brighter than what we shared and I'll never bother you again, though you'll haunt my fantasies the remainder of my days."

She pulled her hand free and rested her fingers on his lips.

He kissed each gloved tip as he waited for her to speak. "Tell me, Lucy. The truth will set us both free."

On the other side of the room, a rush of bodies caught Eliza's attention. Frederick stormed across the ballroom, Sean trying to take his arm but being repeatedly knocked aside like an annoying mosquito.

Eliza stepped out from behind the tree and hurried to Sean.

"I tried, but he began to guess something was going on." Sean tucked her to his side as Frederick reached Alexander and hauled him to his feet with one arm, the other poised to strike.

"No, Freddy. Please don't," Lucy said with calm determination. "He'll leave. He'll leave because there's nothing for him here."

Frederick released Alexander, who moved toward Lucy again. "But do you love him?"

The desperation in Alexander's voice caused Eliza to weaken, but Sean tightened his hold on her.

Lucy dipped her head and angled toward Frederick. "Please go, Alex."

"I'm sorry for all the pain I've caused you," he said in parting.

It took Eliza a moment to recover, then she hurried after her brother with Sean following. "Alex!"

He turned and pulled off his mask. Heartbreak was etched on his countenance, but his eyes were clear. Sober with truth. "Thank you for your help and encouragement, Eliza, but she has Freddy now."

"She never said she loved him! And even if she does, it's not the same way she loves you. She has no passion for him, only fondness."

"Then I pray it's enough for her. She deserves complete love and devotion. I know Freddy will provide it on his end." He ran a hand through his hair. "I can't stay here, but you two enjoy the party. I'll find my way."

"Take the Lyman to get wherever you need to go," she said. "We won't need it for a while." She hoped he understood her implied offer of a nag-free trip to the district.

"Thank you." He smiled and kissed her forehead. "And I'm sure you two will easily claim the prize for being the best dressed couple. Enjoy the attention."

He nodded to Sean and faded into the night.

After giving Eliza a few minutes to regain her composure, Sean escorted her into the ballroom. Rather than trying to make small talk, he led her onto the dancefloor. They spent the better part of an hour waltzing and touching because the darkness allowed heightened explorations.

Later, while she was sitting in a chair awaiting Sean to bring refreshments, the couple in black approached Eliza. Frederick stayed silent—jaw tight—but the still-shrouded Lucy took her hand.

"Freddy heard you did all the paintings. I wanted you to know that I think they're amazing. I hope you have a wonderful life with Mr. Spunner. I've watched you two dancing and can tell you love each other very much." Sean joined them and Lucy nodded to him, though no one could see where she looked. "I was just wishing Eliza and you the best, Mr. Spunner. Congratulations on your engagement and Eliza's fabulous decorations. I'll cherish this night, but I must go."

Frederick started moving toward the door with Lucy, but Eliza impulsively threw her arms about her friend.

"Thank you for all the kind words. I wish you the best as well."

As Eliza and Sean finished their food, Kate Stuart—dressed as a bat in all black with wings jutting out behind both shoulders—arrived with a smile.

"Word is that the woman in mourning was Miss E and she's still brokenhearted over your brother, although FLD is always ready with loving arms."

"I suppose I'll have to wait until the next edition of *Snitch* comes out to know for sure," Eliza quipped.

Kate smiled patronizingly and looked at Sean. "You've caught yourself one with a sharp tongue, Mr. Spunner."

"And a talented tongue it is, Miss Stuart. I wouldn't trade it— or the rest of her—for anything."

He walked them away three steps before Eliza burst into giggles. Arms about her, he smiled. "Are you ready to move on to something more intimate?"

"Always."

Holding hands, they left the ballroom and requested their automobile.

"Eliza, I can't wait any longer. You win our bet."

"Only if I agree to it." She bit her lip and gazed into his eyes—amber under the chandeliers.

His grin doubled. "You *are* a naughty flirt."

"And I'm all yours." She trailed a finger across his jawline. "By the way, I love this look on you—from unshaven face to the breeches. You look like a rake of a duke. Or maybe a baron."

"Then agree with me and I'll allow you to divest me of my fine clothes wherever you wish."

"Anywhere?"

"As per our bet. Whoever begs for it first, the other claims victory by calling the location and position. Remember?"

"It sounds familiar, though it was so long ago I was beginning to believe you didn't know where to stick—"

"Miss Melling, Mr. Spunner. Your driver is out front," a doorman announced.

Eliza took Sean's arm, pressing against him more than necessary on their short walk to the curb.

"Did Alexander get where he needed to go?" she asked the chauffeur when he opened the door to the enclosed back seat.

He smirked—confirming Eliza's suspicions as to the location. "Yes, Miss Melling."

"Thank you. We'll be going to Mr. Spunner's house now." Eliza slipped into the automobile.

"Pull to the back, please," Sean added as he removed his hat.

"Very well, sir."

Normally they would have kissed and touched, but the air of anticipation was too great for Eliza to concentrate on flirtations while the real event loomed on the horizon.

After the automobile was parked, Sean told Eliza to wait in the car while he disappeared inside. He returned a minute later with a sandwich plate and a bottle of cola instead of his top hat and gloves. He handed the food and drink to the driver.

"We might be awhile. Feel free to nap if you can."

"Yes, sir. And thank you."

Sean escorted Eliza into the tidy kitchen. "Sorry for the less-than-grand entrance to my house. One day to be *our* house." He kissed her quickly on the lips. "The cook leaves me a sandwich when I'm out in case I'm hungry when I return, but I thought it best used for your driver. Besides that, there's only one thing I'm hungry for tonight. Where do you want me?"

"Your bedroom, if you please."

"I'm certain I'll be most pleased, Kitten."

He scooped her into his arms. Down a paneled passage, he emerged into a small but grand hall between doors leading to a parlor and formal dining room. After climbing the stairs, he turned left and moved past a few closed doors to enter his lair. He touched the electric switch with his elbow. The space rich in mahogany furniture and blue fabric was illuminated, a shine reflecting off the closed velvet draperies.

Sean set her on the damask bedspread. "What do you think? I've kept things plain for the most part because I want you to choose how to decorate, though the housekeeper has insisted on a few things on the main floor so I don't look a pauper when guests come."

She ran her hands across the smooth bed. "It's perfect, Sean."

He leaned over her, ready to crawl onto the bed.

"No you don't!" Eliza pushed him upright. "My rules."

He gave an exaggerated bow. "And what are your rules, my lady? It can't be anything too scandalous since you've chosen the obvious space of a bedroom."

Eliza pressed her chest against him in a bullying fashion that was too sensual to be intimidating. "For your information, I almost took us to Magnolia Cemetery. Perhaps if we were costumed as vampires or witches instead of in royal silks, I would have."

Startled, his eyes widened. Then his view caught the deep valley of her protruding breast and he dipped low to kiss her there.

She grabbed a handful of hair and yanked his head back. "My rules, Sean Francis Spunner. Remember that or I'll drag you to the cemetery and find a headstone to bed you on."

"You debauched minx! *My* debauched minx with the tits of a goddess." His hair still in her grip, he reached a hand to her breast and trailed his fingers over the swell before tucking them into her cleavage. "It's so tight here tonight, Kitten."

Smiling over his infatuation with her chest, Eliza shoved him back so she could think clearly as she studied his form. "There's no need for you to climax anywhere other than where God intended you tonight. I want the lights kept on and all your clothing removed. Your coat and vest—off!"

She gave him orders as he stripped. Never had they seen each other fully unclothed since they'd worked their explorations and pleasures specific to different areas of their bodies during their brief windows of privacy.

Down to his tented underdrawers, Sean tremored beneath her gaze. "You're killing me, Eliza."

"Good." She smiled as she dropped before him and showed him attentions as she removed his final garment. On her feet a moment later, she stepped back once more. "Now perhaps I'll ask you to pose for me so I can sketch—"

He crushed her in an embrace as his mouth claimed hers. "I'm about to soil your pretty dress, Kitten. I need you."

Loving his exuberance and the pleasure-pain of the rough contact and his scruffy jaw, Eliza gave her next orders. "Carefully remove my clothing."

Gone was all sense of play. Sean's rapt attention projected grim determination and unbridled desire. Completely masculine. Eliza's love burst into a kaleidoscope of feeling from scalp to toes.

When he stepped back to set her final layer over the chair, Eliza pulled out her hairpins. His lustful gaze melted with a look of worshipfulness.

"Eliza Rose," he breathed her name with pure longing. "What a fool I was to wait for this with you."

She opened her arms to him and they surged together in a moment of bliss. The hard planes of his chest pressed against her curves. Hands caressed bare backs. Gentle movements of legs rubbing alongside the other's. And the scent of Sean's cologne on his warm body. Heaven on Earth.

After a few minutes of the exploratory embrace, Eliza tilted her mouth to his ear. "Lie on the bed."

A bed. A soft space to cradle their nakedness. Much better than a quick pounding in an empty room with her skirt flipped up and Edmund's buttons open. Not a stolen moment of teasing in a forest, or a back seat, or the Gulf. *This* was lovemaking. As much as Eliza pretended to be in control, she knew she was in over her head.

And loving every minute of it.

Chapter Fourteen

On November fifth, the Mellings gathered around their ornate dining table for Sunday dinner after late Mass. Eliza picked at the sparse amount of vegetables and meat on the fine china before her, wishing Sean was there to toss an extra roll on her bread plate. He was attending a family dinner celebration, but her mother had forbidden Eliza to accompany him.

"I cannot express how wonderful it is to be without Mr. Spunner today," Ruth said over the roast lamb.

George harrumphed. "Don't be sour, Ruth. Sean is great company."

"I am already tired of him, and we still have the holidays to get through," she said.

Alexander pushed back from the table. "Can't you be happy for one of your children, Mother?"

"I refuse to feign happiness over poor matches and vulgar company."

"There's nothing vulgar about Sean Spunner," Alexander said as he stood. "He speaks the truth and brings joy to your daughter. You should embrace this opportunity to do right after all the wrongs you heaped upon the last love one of your children brought within these walls."

"Get over that bitch already," George sneered. "Clinging to a failed engagement does nothing but enlarge your status of loser. Lucille is gone. The better man won your damaged goods."

Eliza shifted back in her chair when Alexander stormed from the room.

"Stay, Eliza," her father commanded. "I need to discuss the details of the Lavrettas' mural with you."

"I'll have the sketches ready in the morning, Father."

"Show them to me before supper. I need to approve them before your meeting tomorrow, and you might need to rework something."

Eliza bit back the words wanting to slip out and nodded. "I'll bring them to your den this evening, Father."

The remaining three sat through a few more minutes of silence. Ruth excused herself first. When Eliza tried to flee, her father caught her arm.

"Don't forget how important this commission is. Constantine Lavretta is an important man. If you do well, he'll spread your name across clubs and offices for months to come. Not to mention his wife will chatter about your painting—for good or ill—at card parties and social events."

"Yes, Father. I'll do my best not to disappoint you."

"Good girl." He squeezed her shoulder.

Eliza took refuge in her apartment over the garage, locking the door behind her. After opening all the windows to the autumn air, she pulled off her church dress and corset. Tossing the confining clothing aside, she settled in her chemise on a pile of pillows with her sketchbook. Mr. Lavretta had requested a mural of the bay. Eyes closed, Eliza envisioned the sights, sounds, and smells of the ferry ride to Seacliff Cottage. After absorbing all the senses of the water, she opened her eyes and set her pencil racing across the page.

No thoughts of parents.

No pains for Alexander's aching heart.

No anxiety over her father trapping Sean under his thumb.

Knocking—growing louder.

Eliza uncurled from her work and looked about the room. The daylight was dimmer with the advancing afternoon, the tapping insistent.

"Kitten, are you in there?"

Heart in her throat, she managed a *yes* while flipping back through the pad. Four double-spread pages! Legs numb from her prolonged sitting, she stumbled for the door. Sean slipped inside as soon as it opened. Eliza relocked it and fell into his strong arms.

"What happened to the dinner?" she asked.

"Completed, save for post-dinner drinks. It wouldn't be a Finnigan celebration without that, but Megan said I needed a dose of Eliza more than whiskey."

He kissed down her neck as his hands worked over her backside. The instant his mouth met her cleavage, he gripped her hips. Melting into him, she fingered through his hair then tugged off his suit jacket.

"I missed you at dinner."

"Good thing I'm here for dessert."

He had the buttons on the top of her chemise open a second later. She arched under his laving attentions, allowing him to guide her to the floor. Ever since they'd shared the ultimate Halloween night, she'd dreamt of their next time. Of their *every* time. For one night with Sean would never be enough.

"Will you? Here?" She met the wicked grind of his hips with an echoing movement.

Smiling, he looked around the studio. "It's not your family's house, is it?"

She shook her head. "That's way at the other end of the driveway."

"Then it's our lucky day, Kitten." He nipped her chest. "I was hoping you were out here. I came through the Church Street gate rather than go by way of the house."

"Ever the thoughtful one." She untied his red cravat. "I could think of nothing besides removing your clothes during Mass."

He groaned as his hands mussed through her dark tendrils. "I adore you, Eliza. Do you mind if we make love?"

"*Mind?*" She laughed and snaked a hand inside his waistband. "I'd be offended if we didn't."

"I've been in agony remembering our ecstasy on Halloween."

"I'll put you out of your misery, Sean."

Clothes divested, they tumbled on the floor pillows, muffling their vocalizations without speaking of it. Although on the opposite spectrum from her art-induced trance, the mutual pleasuring again wrapped Eliza in a sensual cocoon that left no room for outside worries.

Panting breath, sweating skin.

All focus was on her body and how she connected with her lover.

Exquisite gratification only Sean could give and that she returned in kind.

As they caught their breath after the second round, their entwined limbs flinched when a rapping knock vibrated the door.

"Eliza, are you still at work?" her father called.

"I've worked my fiancé thoroughly this hour," she whispered before nipping Sean's lips.

Wide-eyed, he silently reached for his clothing tossed about the floor, gathering the articles to his naked chest.

"Eliza!" George barked.

"Yes, Father!" She pinched Sean's buttocks, motioned toward her storage room and whispered, "There's a bathroom in there."

She watched him scurry to the other room and kicked her under clothes and corset beneath the pile of pillows while scooping up her dress.

The knob rattled. "Then let me in! I need to see your sketches before supper."

"Coming, Father!" *I did in more ways than one!* She left the top of her dress partially undone and twisted her hair into a hasty bun, pencils stuck through to secure it. She opened the door and stepped to the side. "My legs don't work well after sitting."

George frowned and glanced about the room—the only ornamentations her jumble of bright floor pillows, three easels, and the two-person table and chair set by the miniature kitchen. "You need a drafting table. With more commissions to plan in your future, I can't have you sitting about the floor like a Bohemian. I'll have this apartment decorated properly so you can bring clients here. We'll turn your storage area into a portrait studio, and you may paint the debutantes in the comfort of our own space rather than rushing about town."

Eliza shook her head, though no words escaped.

"This will remain your studio after you marry. Sean will understand and won't feel that he's incapable of providing for you because of your artistic endeavors. Not to mention your mother will only need to cross the lawn to visit you. That might soften the blow she feels with you marrying so young."

"No," she croaked. "This is my private space, but I'll leave once Sean and I—"

"There's no need for further discussion. Plans will be made. Now show me your sketches."

Eliza lifted the tablet from the floor, uncovering Sean's cravat. She shoved it up her sleeve before turning to her father.

Seeming to be in no hurry, he brought the sketchpad to the table and studied each of the pages depicting what would be a panoramic painting to hang in the guest bathroom at the Lavrettas' house.

Pacing the room, Eliza paused over the drying image of a crepe myrtle tree in bloom on one of the easels—a painting she planned to gift to her mother for Christmas.

"Eliza," a rare softness to George's voice made her turn to him. "These are breathtaking. Constantine will be pleased. I'll attend the appointment with you after breakfast."

"Yes, Father."

He put an arm around her shoulders. "Now let's prepare for supper."

"I have a few things to finish before I leave."

George tucked the sketchpad under his arm. "Don't be late. You know your mother hates waiting."

"Yes, Father." She walked him to the door and locked it behind him.

Through the dark storage room she went as though numb, falling against Sean's solid form in the bathroom doorway.

He hugged her to him. "Kitten, I'm afraid I lost my cravat."

She ran her hands over his white shirt before pulling the missing piece from her sleeve and tying it around his neck beneath the poke collar. "Father almost saw it. You won't allow him to keep me imprisoned here after we marry, will you?"

"Of course not. I planned to give you one of the rooms in my house to turn into a studio. Next time you visit, we'll be sure to leave time for you to explore so you may choose which will suit you best."

Snuggled in his arms, Eliza allowed Sean's love to sweep her away once more.

***

On Wednesday, November 22, Claudio waited for the ferry to dock in Daphne. Eliza had written to him, begging the deacon to meet her as she escaped the city. She hadn't sent her typical letters since before Halloween, but she had visited Seacliff two weekends before. She was quiet and stayed home when he and Alexander went riding. Her desperate note arrived Monday, and Claudio could not deny her plea for help.

Eliza rushed off the boat, her traveling cape fluttering behind her like a jewel. After kissing her cheeks, Claudio stepped away.

"What has happened?"

She took his arm and started up the pier. "It's become too oppressive. I had to get away, and you always comfort me."

"But what of Sean? Surely you should cling to your future husband." Tears filled her eyes and Claudio brought her to a stop along the path. "Did he hurt you?"

She shook her head and refused to speak.

"Does your family know you came here?"

"No."

"Then you must go back straightaway."

"There are no more public boats today, and I haven't the cash to pay for a private one. I'll go to Seacliff. Alexander wanted to come this weekend to ride Janus."

"Will there be food in the house to keep you until the Wattses expect your family?"

"I don't know," she said, sobbing. "I don't know anything except that I had to see you."

Claudio put an arm about her and hurried them several blocks to the rectory. He sat with her on the front steps.

"You must tell me what is going on, Eliza." His pulse raced as her blue-violet eyes held his soul in their light.

She took a deep breath and clutched her hands beneath the emerald cape. "I love you. I cannot continue to play at affections for Sean when I always think of you."

It was what he had dreamt of hearing, but it set a block of ice in his chest. He had seen her with Sean and there was no denying their affections. Was it physical only on her part? Had fear of her father's control over Sean driven her to seek an escape? Were the tears in her eyes from her love for a wayward deacon?

"You are unsure, Eliza. You have been worried the past two months and—"

She crushed her lips to his. Claudio responded with passion several seconds then jumped from the steps.

"You cannot—we cannot! You are confused because your relationship with—"

"This isn't about Sean!" she shouted as she bolted for the road.

He chased her, but she was quicker. She ran south and did not slow until they were beyond Daphne's stores and churches. Claudio finally grabbed her arm, forcing her to stop.

Lungs burning, he gasped out the words. "Do not run from me after you begged for help."

Eliza yanked free. "I thought you were different, but you want to control me like everyone else!"

"I only wish to assist you," he said as he followed her down the road.

"You're just like my parents—pushing me so you can gain the most from my actions!" She swung her arms as though shoving aside unseen enemies.

"You must not believe that of me."

"Do you know what I've been doing these past two weeks? A mural! An insipid, pretentious mural in one of Father's client's houses. And guess which room it's in. Guess!" She laughed—a painful rasp of unfamiliar bitterness. "The guest *toilet*. Is my work fit to be admired only by those relieving themselves during a supper party? Maybe I'll get lucky and some couple will hide in there for a quick romp and my scene of Mobile Bay will be enjoyed amid a thrusting session!"

Claudio followed in silence until they approached Montrose, their pace slower for the two miles they covered in the deepening twilight.

"Eliza, shall I try to find you a ride the rest of the way?"

"Don't bother." She looked at him for the first time since her outburst over the mural. "And you don't have to keep following me."

"I will see you safely home where you can create your wonderful art in your special room."

She hugged him and more tears fell. "I'm sorry for doubting you, Claudio. I don't want to lose you."

"I am always here for you, *la mia Rose*." He kissed her cheek.

They walked the final mile holding hands. Darkness enveloped Seacliff Cottage, but a light shone through the front window of the carriage house.

"Wait for me here," she told Claudio at the front gate.

She hurried to the little house by the stable and exchanged words with Mr. Campbell.

"He will have the carriage ready to bring you home in thirty minutes," Eliza informed Claudio as she took his arm and brought him to the front door with the key she'd secured from the coachman.

They turned on the gaslights in the hall and Claudio followed her to the attic. He opened the windows as Eliza stormed back and forth, touching her art supplies and the items in her dresser.

"She's done it again!"

"Who?"

"That maid Father hired. This is the third time I've been here since she began, and I know she's going through my things. Even Mother complained about her. The Watts family is more than capable of keeping things tidy this time of year. We don't need her."

"Do not worry about that tonight." Claudio embraced her. "Rest and I will come tomorrow if you need me."

"Please do." Her lips were like fire upon his jaw. "Come for me, Claudio."

He controlled his faculties enough to walk away and surveyed the state of the kitchen on his way out. Plenty of canned and dried goods, but nothing fresh.

Claudio arranged with Mr. Campbell to collect him in Daphne the following day, and he returned at eight in the morning with pastries, bread, fruit, milk, and butter. The coachman let him in the kitchen door before retreating.

As when he'd first walked into Seacliff Cottage that February day after Mass, the warning not to enter—*Non entrare!*—returned tenfold. Claudio forced himself into the evil atmosphere, placing the groceries away.

"Eliza!" he called after ascending the back stairs to the second floor. "Eliza, I am here!"

She rushed down from the attic and flung herself at him. His arms went about her thin white nightdress, and he kissed her hair until she lifted her face to capture his lips.

He leaned back. "We must move slowly and think things through."

"You came. I love you. You love me. What else is there in life?"

"God, faith, family."

"You will be my family. I have no need for controlling parents full of greed. Even Alex is pushing me toward what he wants."

He gave her a half-smile and smoothed her hair behind her ear. "What could Alexander want from you?"

"He wants me settled—married and safe from scandal so I don't end up like him."

"He wishes to protect you. There is nothing selfish in that."

"But he's pushing me to Sean when what I want is you." She kissed him. "We've played at affections since we met, but it's deeper. You have to feel it, Claudio."

"A fallen deacon would be as much scandal as anything else. I am not worth the trouble it would cause, Eliza."

"I thought you felt the same, but I'm a fool once again!" She ran up the attic stairs and slammed the door.

***

In her room, Eliza took a few calming breaths. It was taking more effort than she'd expected to convince Claudio of her love. She thought it would be easy, that after following her all the way to the attic the previous night he would stay with her. But his ties to the church—the weight of possible sin—was stronger than his feelings for her.

From the top drawer of her dresser, she removed one of her sketches of Sean. After their spectacular time together Halloween night, she'd redressed him in his costume and then torn it apart to capture the sensual image of a Regency rake in disheveled clothing. Kissing the picture, her eyes filled with tears.

"Forgive me," she whispered. "If you do not relent, I need another way out."

Claudio knocked. Calmly, she returned the paper to her drawer and placed her engagement ring on top of it. She allowed tears to stream her cheeks as she opened the door.

"*La mia Rose*, I feel the same as you, but I do not know how to express my love when I am bound to the priesthood."

"I'll show you, *amore mio*." She snuggled against him, trying not to think that he smelled of the incense used during Mass. "Give me today, and if you find no fulfillment, I will not hold you to any promises."

"I cannot—"

Eliza claimed his mouth, tongue searching and hands roaming. He followed her lead, and she arched into his touch as his hands explored. Inch by inch, she backed toward her pallet bed while opening his cassock. She waited until he hit a new level of fervor before lowering to the mattress. Pulling his vestment free, he stepped out of his shoes and lowered on top of her with more kisses.

Eliza worked the buttons of his shirt open. He shivered when her hands trailed his abdomen, but he in turn opened her nightgown.

"Claudio ..." She arched against him—skin to skin—and licked his cheek. "You taste like fear."

It was the final straw on his burden of denied desires. The part of him he had denounced when he'd joined the clergy gained control, and an experienced body took the lead. Eliza couldn't help the tears that continued to fall as she was moved body and soul by the outpouring of love. Only her thoughts kept her grounded as Claudio continued his passionate assault.

I could live with this. I could grow to love this man as he loves me if I'm to leave Sean behind.

She cried out along with him, then lay stunned several minutes. Lest the tears return, she put into play the final touch on her seduction. Sitting, she trailed kisses down his middle.

"Your lines are exquisite, *amore mio*. They beg to be drawn. May I capture you?"

His hand cupped her face, and he leaned in for a deep kiss. "*Sí, la mia Rose.* It is an honor to be part of your talent."

"My muse." From her dresser, she secured a red leather journal that she had planned to save for her honeymoon and returned to the bed with it. "You bring me such joy."

***

That evening, Eliza sat alone in the kitchen with a glass of warm milk and one of the apple pastries Claudio had brought her. Picking apart each flaky layer, she savored the sweetness after a day of bitter emotions while she looked at the engagement ring restored to its rightful place. Hearing someone in the hall, her body tensed.

"Eliza Rose Melling!" George shouted through the house. "I've already spoken to Campbell and know you're here. Come out!"

Eliza walked to the door like a prisoner awaiting a hanging.

The arrogant lift of George's chin and the ice in his eyes reminded Eliza of the times she'd seen Alexander look that way. Assuming a submissive attitude, she lowered her head. "Yes, Father?"

"Why the hell did you leave town without a word? Your mother is in hysterics, and Sean is beyond worried. Of course Ruth told him it was his fault because he indulges you too much, but that's beside the point."

"I'm sorry, Father. I meant to send word today, but I was distracted. I'll write a note so it may be sent on the morning ferry."

"Don't bother. You may explain to Sean in person as he's accompanying Alex here tomorrow afternoon. Your mother and I will be coming as well, but my unnecessary trip today is a nuisance. I went straight to Point Clear to dine and hired a ride to get here."

She didn't know why it bothered him since he'd been making frequent trips across the bay during the past month, but she played her part. "I'm sorry for the trouble, Father."

"Get whatever frivolities you have out of your system over the next few days. I have a portrait consultation scheduled for you on Monday. Your mother cleared your social calendar so you can meet with Mrs. Marley about painting Grace Anne."

"Yes, Father." She turned her back so he wouldn't see her annoyance. Grace Anne Marley was pleasant, but as Lucy's former best friend, the situation had the potential of being awkward. Not to mention it was another forced commission she had no desire to attempt.

"Your involvement in the Halloween Flirts decorations did exactly as I'd hoped in making people aware of your talents. And with Sean as devoted to your artistic endeavors as he is you, you'll have the best of both worlds." He took her arm with fatherly affection, and she turned to him. "I'd never admit this to Alex, but the love he had for Lucille that weakened his common sense I count as a strength in Sean. I want what's best for my daughter, even if it means allowing her husband to be a love-blinded dupe because he needs to be faithful to you."

"A spouse should have the love and fidelity of their partner," Eliza said.

"Dear girl, a husband shouldn't wear out his wife with all his desires. She needs her energy for playing hostess and seeing to the running of the household. I apologize in advance if Sean breaks your stamina, because I won't allow him into the district after the next carnival season. Not that there was much concern to begin with. I've made inquiries and was told that he hasn't been one for frequent liaisons. And since he started courting you, he's had no indiscretions. That should make you pleased."

Eliza could only stare at the monster she was forced to call Father.

"Don't look shocked, Eliza. There's no need to continue to coddle your delicate feminine sensibilities. I'll be sure your mother has the talk with you before long so the act on your wedding night isn't a complete shock." He stroked her hair. "Daughters *are* challenging to educate. With sons, it's just the exchange of money with a professional. Sleep well, dear. I leave early for the ferry."

Angst pulsed through her from the filth he'd spewed. To release it, she spent hours painting an image of her hellish father before she could attempt to settle for the night.

Chapter Fifteen

Eliza woke chilled not long after dawn. Pulling on her robe, she went down the back stairs to prepare coffee. While waiting for the water to boil, a moan echoed down the hall. On bare feet, she crept toward the entry. A light shone around the door to her father's den because it wasn't completely shut. Creeping closer, Eliza held her breath.

"Oh, George!"

"Take it! Take everything I give you and beg for more!"

"Yes! Give—"

A scream that sounded more pain than pleasure split the words as the thumping of furniture soured Eliza's stomach. She retreated to the kitchen, shoved back the things she'd gotten out, and ran for the attic.

She huddled in bed all morning, ignoring hunger pains and thirst. At noon, a knock sounded on her door.

"Miss Eliza?" Rosemary called. "I heard you were here and hate to see you miss a meal. I brought you a tray."

"Come in!" Eliza gave the cook her first smile of the day. "And thank you. I did miss breakfast, but how did you know I was here?"

"Lydia, the new maid." Rosemary set the tray on the side of the bed. "She got here before Mr. Melling left and he told her."

"I wonder if he told her before or after he bedded her."

"For shame, Miss Eliza! A young lady like you doesn't need to speak like that."

Eliza sipped the coffee. "It's true. That's why I've stayed up here. I don't want to see what trollop my Father is cheating on my mother with."

"You can't hide from her forever. She'll be up here soon."

"I don't want her in my room! She's been touching my things and—"

"How else can someone dust, Miss Eliza?"

"She doesn't need to pillage my drawers to dust! Tell her she's not allowed in here. I'll clean myself rather than have her greedy hands spoiling my things."

"She isn't one to take direction from me. You'll need to tell her yourself."

Eliza ate and showered. While she dressed midafternoon, a knock sounded. Boldly crossing the attic in nothing but her underthings topped with a bustier, she opened the door. The curly-haired brunette standing two steps down the stairwell couldn't have been much older than herself. She took in the sight of Eliza with a shocked expression.

"Excuse me, Miss, but I'm here to clean your room. I'm—"

"I know who you are and I don't wish your services."

"Have I been unsatisfactory?"

"Most definitely! You're not allowed in my room—ever. Do you understand?"

"Yes, Miss." Lydia looked at her feet.

"Not even if my mother or father orders you to clean in here."

Her eyes widened. "But I can't disobey an order from Mr. Melling if I wish to keep my job."

"Is that what you told yourself when *Mr. Melling* had his way with you? You had to obey orders to commit adultery this morning to keep your measly job?"

Lydia went red, her eyes narrowed. "No, *Miss Eliza*, I came early this morning because George sent an invitation to me last night to join him. I guess thoughts of me made him overlook a pesky problem like his daughter being in the house." Her tone matched Eliza's vehemence.

"Keep your filthy hands out of my room or I'll see you jailed for your actions!"

Eliza slammed the door in Lydia's face and fell onto a pile of pillows. Reaching for her main sketchbook, she flipped to an empty page and drew the sharp-nosed maid with a crow's beak pecking at all Ruth Melling's jewels.

***

Hours later, Eliza lounged on her stomach in the middle of her floor, sketching Sean as he'd looked at the Gulf on the Fourth of July—shirtless and virile amid the waves. Still wearing only underclothes, Eliza's décolletage was displayed to its best advantage with the lifting shapewear as she propped on her elbows. When a knock came, she knew who it would be and called for him to enter.

Sean's smile was as broad as the bay when he set his lusty gaze on her.

"Lock the door," she commanded.

"But Alex—"

"He's showering, isn't he? That's what he does when he comes home. And my parents?"

"They went on to the hotel for supper."

"They'll not be back until late tonight." Eliza flashed her best come-hither smile. "So, as I said, Mr. Spunner, lock the door."

He hastily complied and then dropped to his knees before her, sitting back on his haunches. Looking at the sketchbook, his smile doubled. "Thinking of me, Kitten?"

"Always, Sean." She leaned up for a kiss, and his hands were immediately upon her chest as their tongues tangoed. She got to her knees and went for his trousers.

He hissed in a breath. "You know how I feel about being a guest in your parents' house."

"Who do you love more—me or my father?"

"You. You know I do." He squeezed her breasts simultaneously.

She arched into his touch. "Only because my father doesn't have glorious tits."

"Don't even tease, Eliza. You know I'd go mad without you."

"Then make love to me, Sean. Show me you forgive me for leaving town without telling you. I'll do all I can to help ease any bruises to your ego." She rubbed her chest against him. "You can start here for old time's sake, but you know where I'll want you to complete."

Eliza was glad he set to work adjusting the floor pillows rather than bringing her to the bed. Her sheets still held the faint scent of incense from the shared hours with Claudio the day before, and she didn't wish to remember the desperation she felt in order to escape her parents. For now, she hoped Sean's breaking his rule about sex in one of her family's houses proved how far he was willing to cross George Melling in order to please her. Momentarily set free, Eliza relished the give and take of their harmonized appetites.

Afterward, she snuggled against his broad chest. "We should run away together."

His warm hand rubbed down her back, pressing her into him. "We can't do that."

"A romantic Christmas in the Smoky Mountains after a wedding in some little chapel along the way would be excellent. A cabin with a large hearth and a soft rug." She kissed his neck.

"Your mother is set on a cathedral wedding. I haven't been on my best behavior all these months only to elope and bring her wrath upon me."

"What about what I want?" She sat up although she didn't want to lose his delicious contact. "I've lived my whole life under my parents' oppressive ideals. I want to cling to you and no one else. Believe me when I say they'll make our lives miserable. You can't join Melling and Associates. We have to get away!"

"Shh, Kitten." He brought her into his arms. "You've had a stressful few weeks with the mural, and—"

"I never wanted that job!" She pushed away. "I don't aim to waste my time painting bathrooms or silly debutantes. That's what Father's pushing me to next—portraits for spoiled girls wishing to capture a rich husband. I'm an artist, not an animal trained to perform on command. I paint and draw what moves me—not what's forced. That isn't art of flesh and blood. That's cold machinery. It'll bleed me dry, Sean. There'll be nothing left in me for my self-portraits or these sketches of you from our glorious times together. I fear I'll be too emotionally shriveled to have any passion to give. Then what type of wife and lover would I be?"

"You're the best lover." He urged her back into the pillows and nibbled her lips.

"And I want to stay that way." She stroked him. "Don't let them suffocate me. We need to be free. Save me, Sean."

His desire washed over her like a cleansing rain as he urged her to new heights. Arms and legs wrapped around him, she held to his unspoken promises as their passion soared. Eliza's return was a dizzying descent through immobility and blindness.

"Don't tell me I broke you, Kitten."

She smiled, eyes still closed. "In all the best possible ways."

Alexander's voice called through the locked door. "Eliza, have you captured our guest?"

"Yes!" She giggled as Sean poked her with his toes.

"Don't let him in," he whispered.

"He knows what we're doing. Pull on your pants and toss me a blanket."

Sean did as instructed and opened the attic door. Alexander strode inside, taking in the sight of his sister on a nest of pillows, her bare shoulders peeking out of the blanket. His eyes cut back to shirtless Sean by the door in rumpled trousers.

"I'd apologize for interrupting, but you both have the glow of people who already enjoyed a good frolic."

Eliza laughed as she watched him circle the room. "*So* good!"

"Supper will be announced in fifteen minutes," Alexander said. "That should give you enough time to dress." He paused before the easel that faced away from the sitting area. "This is brilliant, Eliza. Though I'm sorry for whatever event spurred you to capture it."

Sean crossed the room and stood open-mouthed beside Alexander, studying the angry painting of reds and purples depicting George Melling as a demon.

Eliza hugged the blanket to her torso as the emotions washed over her once more.

"Father's having Sean watched to make sure he doesn't cheat on me, stacking commissions so I can climb the social ladder, and screwing the new maid. She's not even trying to keep it a secret." With pleading eyes, she looked at Sean. "I can't continue to live like this."

Understanding lit his intelligent eyes. "I'll see what I can do."

But will it be enough?

***

After supper, the three gathered in the parlor for drinks. Alexander and Sean both wore tuxedo pants, vests, and bowties but left off their tailcoats. Eliza had on a red tea gown and not a stitch of undergarments. She loved the delicious feel of the silk directly on her skin and Sean's frequent attentions as he explored her natural form—both above and beneath the dress.

"As soon as Father and Mother return, I'm done pretending chaperone duties." Alexander puffed out a smoke ring.

"But you're the best chaperone, Alex." Eliza trailed her hand over Sean's thigh as she rested against him.

"Because I turn the other cheek while you two take what you want. It's painful to witness your affections while I'm starved for my true love." He leaned back in the chair. "I wish I could have seen under her veil at the Halloween dance. Her voice is haunting me as it is."

"I'm sure the vision of you in that body suit and your kissable lips on display are fueling Lucy's fantasies." Eliza ran a finger down Sean's arm.

Alexander gave a waggish smile and adjusted himself. "I did look dashing, didn't I? But a sapling compared to swashbuckling Freddy."

"How many times do I need to tell you she doesn't love him romantically?"

"As many times as needed until she's in my arms once more."

"Then I'll continue to do so, Alex."

A companionable silence filled the room, allowing the sound of the approaching carriage to be heard. Eliza pressed in for a deep kiss from Sean before they separated several inches on the settee.

The front door opened and footsteps accompanied by a muffled sob went directly up the stairs. A moment later, the man of the house filled the doorway.

"Ruth hopes you will all forgive her. She's not feeling well and doesn't wish to be poor company." George's gaze settled on his son. "You should have accompanied us, Alex. The Stuart family was there, and Kate is a striking creature."

Alexander choked on his brandy. After the coughing subsided, he scoffed. "You can't be serious. She hates me, and I'm none too fond of her."

"It's people like that you need to keep close," George said. "Even when she gives up that silly gossip magazine, she'll still be a force to be reckoned with. When you see her at Christmas parties next month, be sure to pay her compliments."

"The hell I will!" Alexander glared at his father before softening enough to give Eliza and Sean a nod. "It was a pleasant evening, but I'm going to my room. Goodnight."

George helped himself to a shot of whiskey and took his chair. "Is everything settled between the two of you after Eliza's hasty flight from town?"

"Yes, sir." Sean shifted closer to Eliza while keeping eye contact with the man across from him. "And we've discussed some things this evening. I believe Eliza's talents would be better served by allowing her to set her own projects. Her creativity might begin to suffer if she's only working on paintings that others must approve of."

"What is art other than seeking approval for a job well executed?" George said. "An artist creates then places it on display to hear what a wonderful job they did. There's nothing stifling about being paid to create something for someone to display in their home. The more projects she does, the more people will learn of her, and the possibilities of her having time to explore will increase over the years. She needs to gather admirers while she's young and a novelty."

He left no room for debate in his self-assured ramblings. If Eliza hadn't known better, she might have been convinced of his brilliance herself.

"Perhaps more time in between the commissions would—" Sean began.

"She'll have had nearly a week by the time she meets the Marleys on Monday. How industrious do you think she'll be with more time than that between paying clients? On her first free day she fled across the bay to avoid work." He looked at his daughter. "What have you occupied your time with since you ran away? Art or idleness?"

Eliza wanted to blurt out that she'd been having sex, but instead she lifted her chin. "I've completed one canvas and over a dozen sketches of my own choosing."

George took in the information of being proven wrong, but after a moment's pause, he threw it back. "When Eliza is driven, there will be no stopping her creativity—with or without paying work she must attend to first."

Sean wasted no time with the next complaint. "There's something else I've wanted to mention, Mr. Melling. I believe it would best serve everyone if I stay with my uncle's firm, even after the wedding."

Eliza's floundering heart grabbed at the seed of hope as her father stared at Sean.

"My uncle has planned for me to become a senior partner when I turn thirty and then take over when he's ready to retire," Sean continued. "My chance of something similar happening at your firm is slim, what with Alexander already established there with a claim through kinship."

George stood and took his final swig of whiskey. "Do you mean to tell me how to run my business, Sean?"

"No, sir."

"Then don't presume anything. For all you know, I might have plans to take in you and your uncle and change the name to Melling, Spunner, Finnigan, and Associates. I might look at court cases, personal life and aptitude in the decision to award the best man—blood son or not —a full partnership." He stood before the settee. "Goodnight to the both of you. Please don't keep my daughter up too late, Sean."

Before Eliza could air her frustration, her father paused in the doorway.

"And remember, Sean, you and your uncle might have issues growing your practice if you're in competition with me." He ascended the stairs.

"Of all the—"

Sean quieted Eliza with a kiss, but she fled through the front door in her bare feet with Sean at her heels. Once she was on the cold sand of the beach, his white sleeves were around her red dress.

"He thinks he owns us, but I'll not be controlled!"

"Shh, Kitten." He nipped her ear and shifted his grip so that he pressed against her chest. "Your father can't control everything. He can't control our passion."

"We have to elope! Let's go tomorrow—anywhere but New Orleans or Atlanta where Father has extended family. The mountains, like I said before! Please take me away from here," she begged.

He nuzzled against her neck. "If we leave, he'll take it out on my uncle's firm, and I can't ruin his life when he brought me into his home after my parents died. We'll have to stay and fight for our freedom."

"We'll never win." Eliza's knees weakened and Sean let her crumble to the sand but followed her down.

"I'll protect you."

She shook her head and touched his cheek. "You'd have to be as ruthless and cold as he is."

"And you don't think I can do that?"

"You're a giving lover, Sean. It's not in your nature."

It was too dark to see what color his eyes shone, but they narrowed and his voice turned husky. "What do I need to do to prove I can protect you?"

"Father respects callousness in others. The only way he might relent is if you prove to be selfish and hard."

His broad smile was tinged with a touch of maliciousness as he grabbed her hips. "I'm hard all right, Eliza. And I'll selfishly take my pleasure with you."

"Yes, please!"

He guided her to her hands and knees, unadorned skin bared beneath her gown. The gentle lapping of the bay was drowned by the sounds of Sean's thrusting. He gave her no physical contact other than his grasp on her hips that kept her where he wished, but his erotic control brought her to ecstasy.

I'll miss this, Sean—my lover. Remember that I've given you my passion and no one else. It will never be like this with Claudio.

WINTER

Chapter Sixteen

For the third time in as many weeks, Claudio walked to Seacliff Cottage to meet Eliza. He had promised to have finalized plans for their January elopement by New Year's. She would visit him after Christmas so he could tell her the details, leaving no letter of evidence.

After the Thanksgiving meal the Mellings shared with Sean's family, Eliza had told Claudio she had officially broken her engagement—which would explain her unrest and sadness since then. He did all he could to bring her healing with their shared moments, but she only looked peaceful when drawing. Claudio posed for her sketches both before and after they made love. If he happened to fall asleep, he woke to her studying him as her pencil moved across the page—a sound he had grown to cherish.

As arranged, he let himself in the front door and unbuttoned his cassock as he climbed the stairs to the attic. Although it was cold, Eliza had all the dormer windows open, and she sat on the floor in her undergarments with a sketchpad.

"*Buongiorno, la mia Rose.*"

She snapped the book shut and looked up. "Claudio!"

The morning sun caught her brilliant eyes as she smiled. There was moisture in them, but she tried to blink it away.

"What is it?" He slipped the frock from his shoulder and hung it on one of the hooks by the door.

She tucked the sketchpad she'd been using under a pillow and held her hands out to him as he approached. "If Alex invites you to go riding with him, don't accept."

He caressed her porcelain face and softly kissed her lips. "Why not? I would like to spend as much time with him as possible before we leave next month."

"I'm afraid I won't be able to hide my feelings for you, and it's too early for Alexander to know about our plans." Eliza raised his hand to her heart. "Promise me you won't go."

"He already sent me an invitation to join him at noon tomorrow."

Eyes wide with fear, she crushed his hands. "Did you accept?"

"He expects me without a reply. I have never let him down."

"You must this time." She released his hands and fidgeted with the finger that used to hold her engagement ring. "Write a note of regret before you leave and place it in his bedroom."

"And this will bring you peace?"

"Yes."

"Then I will do it."

His mouth went to hers. It could have been his imagination, but she felt stiff beneath his ministrations. Hoping to ease her worries, he gently kissed her. She melted under his touch, opening to him and pressing closer for more. When he lowered her to the pillows and his finger hooked the waistband of her underwear, she stilled.

"No, Claudio. I don't want to today."

He kissed her in a motion of blessing—forehead, center, and each breast. "Are you worried over our plans? I have spoken with a parishioner who has family in New York. He believes they would be willing to help a young couple gain their footing in a new city. I have written to them about a lovely young artist and her husband who would like to become a chef needing a temporary place to stay when they arrive because they have lost their family here. I should hear before Christmas if they can give us placement, then we can pick the best train schedule."

"New York! Oh, Claudio, that's perfect! No one will find us there." She knocked him to the floor with her exuberance.

Feeling the joy and relief coursing through her body, he laughed. "*Sí*, there is no need to worry."

"It's so much better than Sean's plan." She whispered the words, but they pierced his heart.

Is she comparing me for my excellence or has she only picked me because I can get her further away from her parents?

His hands went to her waist. "Eliza?"

She smiled and raised her eyebrows. "Claudio."

The name rolled from her tongue as a verbal caress.

"Shall I make love to you now that you are not worried?"

She adjusted a few of the floor pillows and snuggled into his arms. "Just hold me today, *amore mio*. I fear the afterglow will be too noticeable to my family when they arrive this evening."

Embracing her, he breathed in her floral scent. "You complete me as well, *la mia Rose*. The glow of our hours together and the joy it produces is difficult to contain."

So comfortable was he with Eliza, Claudio fell asleep. For the first time upon waking, he found her slumbering as well. The sun coming through the windows proved it to be midday. He kissed her forehead to rouse her.

She sat upright. "The time! Rosemary will be looking to feed me dinner. You must go!"

She hastily pulled on one of her cotton dresses he loved to see her in and nodded to her writing desk. "And don't forget the letter to Alex. Use the plain stationery in the right drawer. He'll never know it's mine."

Several minutes later, Eliza led the way down the attic stairs as Claudio buttoned his cassock. She paused in the second floor hallway as he placed the letter in Alexander's room, then she motioned him to follow. Halfway down the main staircase, a uniformed maid emerged from the parlor and looked up at them—first with surprise and then a knowing smirk.

"Thank you for bringing your letter, Deacon De Fiore," Eliza said as she reached the foyer. "Alex will be sure to see it since you placed it in his room."

She ignored the staring maid and walked with Claudio as far as the gate. Rather than embracing him, she clasped her hands behind her back.

"Please don't seek me out these next few weeks, Claudio. It's a sensitive time for me—for us. I'll send word to you before New Year's on when to meet me."

"But what of my Christmas gift for you?"

"We'll have many Christmases together in the future. This sacrifice must be made to keep our plans secret." She touched a hand to his as she leaned in for quick kisses on the cheek. "Have a Merry Christmas, *amore mio*. I'll see you as soon as I can."

Claudio made his way back to Daphne with the ghost of Eliza's lips on his face.

***

Saturday morning, Claudio worked alongside fishermen from the parish as he helped haul their sunrise catch from a boat at the Daphne pier. The physical work in the brisk winter air was invigorating, as was the boisterous conversations in his native tongue. Claudio's mind turned to Eliza—how he needed to teach her more Italian than just terms of endearment so that she could get along better in the community and church they would be living among in New York.

"Deacon, stay alert or go home!" a man shouted in Italian.

Claudio laughed and stepped away from the action until he could clear his head of Eliza. He wiped his hands on the heavy apron he wore over his rolled shirtsleeves and daydreamed of being similarly clad in a restaurant kitchen. Food of his homeland—it filled the soul almost as well as the gospel. He could enrich people's lives with savory meals, help them smile and relax after a busy day. Then he would return home and fulfill the needs of his wife. *Una vita perfetta!*

From down the beach, a wild, trilling shout he often heard Alexander exclaim was followed by an echoing one. Eliza called it the "Rebel yell."

Alexander tore across the sand on Janus. Flora wasn't far behind, but rather than carrying Eliza, the horse was ridden by Sean Spunner. Knowing the hasty ride north would be followed by a return trip south, Claudio left the pier to wait in the sand.

Several minutes later, the riders returned at a slower pace. Claudio waved his arms at their approach, and Alexander reined Janus to stop.

"Claudio!" He dismounted and greeted his friend. "Are you now a fisher of fish rather than of men?"

"I do what I can to help the parishioners."

"You missed an exciting ride to Spanish Fort." Alexander turned to Sean as Flora came to a halt behind him. "Sean knows how

to push the limits with Flora as well as her owner." The friends
laughed.

"I am surprised to see you here," Claudio remarked to Sean.
"Are you well since—"

"De Fiore!" A shout came from the pier, requesting
assistance.

"Excuse me, but I am needed."

"No worries, Claudio," Alexander said. "I'll see you later.
Stop by tomorrow since today is too busy for you."

"Yes, I'm sure Eliza would enjoy it," Sean said.

Claudio nodded and returned to his duties, worrying over the
meaning of Sean's being a guest of the Mellings.

He worked the next hours preparing fish for a parish feast to
be held that evening. Midafternoon, a letter arrived at the rectory
from Seacliff Cottage while he chopped onions. He washed his hands
and settled by the fireplace to read.

> *Dear Claudio,*
> *Alex told me he saw you on the beach in*
> *Daphne. It must have been a shock for you*
> *to see him with Sean—it was to me when he*
> *came home with him yesterday evening. You*
> *know my brother has pushed for my union*
> *with him. Alex was highly upset when I*
> *broke off the engagement and has been trying*
> *to reunite us ever since. I had the feeling he*
> *would bring him, which is why I did not wish*
> *you to visit this weekend. It would be*
> *awkward for all of us, and my heart cannot*
> *handle the potential confrontation.*
> *Let us keep to our previous arrangements*
> *and be happy for what the future holds—*
> *freedom!*
> *Love,*
> *Your Devoted Rose*

The unease he'd felt all day dispersed with the simple
explanation. Sean was Alexander's friend, someone to whom Claudio
knew he wanted his sister to marry. There was nothing to stop
Alexander from trying to bring them back together because he did
not know of his other friend's entanglement with Eliza. Alexander

was not to blame for placing her ex-fiancé as a temptation before her. He knew not what he did, but Claudio would pray she would remain devoted to her true love.

Chapter Seventeen

At Christmas dinner, Eliza enjoyed the splendor of the Government Street mansion knowing that such luxuries as china, crystal, and the finest foods would soon be extinct to her. Patrick, Cecelia, and Megan Finnigan—Sean's uncle, aunt, and cousin—took post-supper drinks in the morning room with her parents and when Alexander disappeared, the couple was left alone at the dining table.

"Are you ready for your present?" Eliza's new gown of emerald velvet showcased her curves, and she shifted enticingly beside Sean.

"You already gave me the splendid cufflinks." He fingered the gold bracelet he'd given her on the portico before midnight Mass the night before.

She kissed him. "I mean the real gift—the one you'll have to sneak home while our families aren't looking."

His grin made her heart soar. "I didn't know there was such a thing, Kitten. Shall I expect a similar gift every year, or is it a pre-wedding special?"

"That depends on several things, but let's see how you like it first."

They crossed the yard to her studio above the garage. As soon as she was in her space, she kicked off her heeled slippers and led Sean into the middle of the room. She kissed him, long and deep, while his hands trailed her hips.

"Now close your eyes and wait here. It isn't wrapped."

"I hope that means you'll be unwrapped when you bring it to me."

She leaned in for another kiss and then rested her forehead against his chest. "I love you."

"And I love you. Look, my eyes are closed."

She laughed and swallowed the threat of tears as she went to the back room where she kept her finished canvases. Carefully unearthing it from where it lay facing the wall behind four other paintings, she lifted the self-portrait. The framed painting was four feet tall and showcased in life-sized glory her unbound hair trailing her back, bare above a dipping purple sheet that flashed a peek of her derriere. Her image was turned sideways to look behind, a seductive smile on her lips and her eyes burning with passion for the one she looked upon, while a hand cupped the sheet to her breast.

Heart pounding, Eliza carried it into the front room and leaned it against her middle, facing Sean.

"Open your eyes."

He practically shed tears of joy as he fell to his knees. "Eliza, you're brilliant—both in form and talent. To hell with what your father does. I'll hang this in my office and be the most popular lawyer in the city!"

They laughed and Eliza knelt to join him on the floor, carefully setting the painting aside. "I want you to remember me when we're parted. Never forget me, Sean."

"You've made the likelihood of that impossible." His fingers trailed the swell of her chest and snaked around her neck to draw her in for a kiss.

After several minutes of attention, Eliza broke their contact. "I wanted to let you know I'm going to Seacliff on Saturday. I'll go on the morning ferry and come back that evening."

"Alone?"

"I want to bring some of my new clothes over and collect a few canvases that weren't dry enough for transportation last time."

"I'd be happy to assist you."

"I appreciate it, but don't you have the final fitting for your New Year's tuxedo Saturday afternoon?"

"Yes, but—"

"But what? Have I not earned your trust? Don't tell me you'll be a jealous husband."

His hands splayed over her hips and tugged her into an embrace that stirred everything to life within her body.

"I had a dream last night. Megan always teased me about having second sight like an Irish witch because I've dreamt of other loved ones before their deaths. I don't want to lose you."

"You're the farthest thing from an old hag, Sean Francis Spunner." Eliza kissed him, then smiled. "How did I die in your dream?"

His grip trailed her waist. "An accident on Flora—she threw you."

"Flora is as gentle as they come, but I promise not to go riding this time. Will that make you feel better?"

"Yes, Kitten. Thank you." He nipped at her décolletage. "I'll miss you and these beauties. Shall I collect you at the dock Saturday evening?"

"That would be wonderful."

***

Saturday morning, Eliza followed Claudio and Mr. Campbell up the Daphne pier as they carried one of her trunks. Once it was strapped on the back of the carriage, Claudio helped Eliza into the coach and climbed in after her.

"I'm glad Alex came yesterday evening and invited you today," she said. "This gives us the perfect time to—"

Claudio pressed his lips to hers. "*Felice Natale, la mia Rose.* That is your Merry Christmas kiss, and here is your gift."

He pulled a small parcel from his cassock and placed it in her hands with a beaming smile. Unable to refuse it—and embarrassed that she had not thought to get him something—Eliza put all her energies into opening it. Under the brown paper and a few layers of raw cotton lay a dainty gold crucifix of notable workmanship.

"It's lovely, Claudio. Thank you. I'm afraid you'll have to wait until we get to Seacliff for yours."

"Spending time with you is the best gift of all. May I place it on you?"

Eliza nodded and turned her back to him. Arms about her with the open clasp in his fingers, he fastened it at the nape of her neck, leaving a gentle kiss below her hairline. Facing him once more, she shivered at the intensity in his dark eyes.

"Now the two things I love and honor most are together. God has truly blessed me." His mouth crushed hers with a searing kiss that swept within for more.

Eliza responded—what else could she do? But tears streaked her cheeks.

Claudio straightened and wiped the moisture with his thumbs. "Tears of joy, Eliza Rose. I feel the same."

She sniffed. "Tell me the plans before we reach the house."

"On the night of January 10th we need to be at the Spanish Fort train station. Arturo Perazzo and his family will expect us at their home in Greenwich Village the day our train arrives in New York City. He says he will help me secure work, the parish of Our Lady of Pompeii will welcome us with open arms, and there is a growing art community that will help your creative endeavors flourish."

A thousand miles of separation from my parents and a thriving art community! I might love him for this one day.

She fell upon him with conviction for the first time in months. He responded to her passion with fervor of his own—caressing her curves and holding her to him as the carriage rocked.

"Eliza, marry me today. We could slip away for a few hours so it will be official and we will not have to travel unwed. We can arrive in New York properly as husband and wife."

Clinging to him, she shook her head. "Not today, Claudio. We can stop along the way and be married once we get into Virginia or beyond. Somewhere my parents can't stop us. It's only eleven more days."

Claudio nodded and kissed her hair.

***

On Tuesday, January 9th, Eliza closed her traveling case and left it in the marble foyer of the Government Street mansion. Going to her mother in the morning room, she spoke without waiting.

"I'm stopping at the office to speak with Alex before we leave, Mother. Could you pick me up there on the way to the ferry?"

Ruth appraised her daughter's wool traveling suit. "Make sure you are ready for me."

"Yes, Mother. And I left my case in the foyer." She gave her a rare show of affection with a quick kiss on the cheek. "Thank you for coming with me. I don't want to continue to worry Sean with my midweek flights from the city."

"I don't like to think of you missing two masquerades by staying at Seacliff four nights, but despite his many faults, Sean understands your creative needs."

"He'll join us Friday evening along with Alex, and we can have our own party after supper. That new black-and-cream gown you bought me for Christmas will do well. It was in the trunk I took across the bay the other week."

Ruth nodded. "I'll pack a few masks, but go on, Eliza. I am sure you'll want to stop at Sean's office as well."

Eliza nodded, though she had no intention of speaking with Sean before leaving. They had shared a glorious lunch hour at his home the day before, and she intended to keep that her last vision of him—his flesh in all its magnificence as he filled her for the final time.

Unless she was caught.

If she was stopped at any point in their flight, she would claim Claudio had seduced her and return to Mobile in real tears because part of her would be relieved to come back to Sean. That was why she had to enlist Alexander's help with her plan. Alex had to think her love for Claudio was stronger than her desire to leave their parents. He was too much of a romantic fool to allow her to do so without believing in her complete adoration for the Italian.

At Melling and Associates, the bumbling secretary in the main waiting room gave her a nervous smile.

"Good afternoon, Miss Melling."

She nodded and continued up the stairs where Alexander's secretary sat respectfully at her desk, graying hair in a tidy bun.

"Hello, Miss Renna," Eliza greeted the woman she'd known since birth.

"Miss Eliza! How can I help you today?"

"I'm here to see Alex if he has a few minutes to spare."

Miss Renna checked the clock. "You're in luck. His last appointment just left, but he doesn't leave for the courthouse for another thirty minutes. Shall I announce you?"

"Thank you, but I'd rather surprise him."

Eliza eased through the partially open door and closed it behind her. Alexander looked over from where he sat on his desk— feet on the bookcase under the window and a flask to his lips. She crossed the office and hugged him before reaching for the drink.

"I keep thinking that if I stare long enough, she'll materialize on her favorite bench." He took one more swig after Eliza, then he closed the flask. "She used to love sitting in the park, but now she never leaves home."

"She came to the Halloween Flirts dance," Eliza reminded him. "And I've heard she's attended a few shows, sitting in the back and leaving early."

"All with Frederick." Alexander shook his head. "It's been a year, but it hurts like it was yesterday."

"You wouldn't wish that pain on anyone, would you?"

"Never."

"People should follow their love, no matter where it leads or who they leave behind."

"We need to cling to our heart's true mate and forget the rest."

Eliza took her brother's hands. "Will you support me when I do that, Alex? I need to know you're on my side."

"You know I am. Sean and you are—"

"I'm not in love with Sean. I might have been infatuated to a degree, but my passion is with my muse."

"Your muse?"

"I knew as soon as I saw his features in the little chapel that—"

"Dear God, Eliza! Claudio?" He looked incredulous.

"You had to warn me away from him, remember? I wanted to touch and be with him from the beginning, but you put Sean in front of me. I *tried*. I tried to love the more respectable choice, but my heart can no longer handle it."

"He'll be a priest within the year, Eliza! You can't harbor a love affair with—"

"We're to be married and are escaping from here." She put on her best smile as tears welled in the corner of her eyes. "But I need your help. Will you help me, Alex? Help true love fly from our poisonous parents so it can live free and grow?"

Alexander touched her cheek, unspoken questions in his pale blue eyes.

"I need you to keep my secret, but I had to tell you now because there won't be privacy once we're at Seacliff. Don't tell Sean or anyone. I'll break things to him gently this weekend. Claudio and I aren't going away until next week, so there will be time to soothe everyone from the broken engagement before they know of the elopement. Will you keep that secret, Brother? You're the only one who can begin to understand what I've suffered under our parents and what pain comes from denying love."

He nodded. "If you truly love each other."

"Ask him yourself." Eliza smiled though it hurt her to lie to Alexander. "He's been the muse I always hoped for. I filled a journal with scandalous pictures of him that he's now embarrassed over. I need your help with that as well."

"How so?"

"The book reminds Claudio of our sin because we are not yet married. I can't take it with us and cause him fresh pain. I need it destroyed, and I'll have no opportunity to do so while Mother is with me this week. Will you burn it for me after we leave?"

"If it will help Claudio."

"And me!" Eliza kissed his smooth cheek. "It's a red leather sketchbook, hidden on top of the toilet tank in my bathroom. And, Alex, if for some reason Father or Sean or anyone catches on to our plans, please destroy it immediately. No good would come of it being discovered."

"I will, Eliza Rose."

"You promise?"

He nodded and embraced her. "I'll miss you. I'll miss you both."

"We'll write and send for you once we're settled."

Eliza left her brother's office with a pleased smile. The sketchbook was the only problem in her plan, making Alexander's role as important as anything else. She could not bring the book with her, because if they were caught she couldn't have evidence of her play upon the deacon. But it was needed to prove to her brother that she'd been in a relationship with Claudio. With his promise to handle the issue, Alexander left her free to leave all cares behind.

Chapter Eighteen

On the chosen day of January 10, 1906, Claudio went to Seacliff Cottage to take tea with Eliza and her mother. Mrs. Melling was her usual aloof self, only present in the conversation to find fault in the subject of discussion. The stress of their departure that night had Eliza tremoring in her white gloves, an odd thing for her to wear. After settling her rattling teacup on its saucer, her mother gave her a sharp look.

"You're quite unwell today, Eliza. You should lie down after Claudio leaves."

"But I wanted to ride Flora. I missed that on my last visit because I promised Sean I wouldn't ride."

"Perhaps later. For now you need rest."

Toward the end of the tea, Eliza brought up the ploy they had agreed upon to secure her luggage for their travel. It wasn't much, but she would have to make do until they arrived in New York.

"Claudio, I spent some time this morning going through my wardrobe and dresser," she said. "There are several items I no longer wish to keep. Do you have ladies in your parish who are in need?"

"*Sí*, Father Angelo is good about finding homes for things when donations come in."

"Do pass along those hideous wash dresses," Mrs. Melling drawled.

"I've packed a suitcase with the unwanted things," Eliza said. "Would you be a dear and bring them back with you to be dispersed, Claudio?"

"I would be happy to, Eliza."

"Only if at least one cotton dress goes along with it." Mrs. Melling adjusted the collar of her tea gown.

"There are two included, Mother."

"Good. Now say goodbye so you can rest. Claudio may accompany you to your room to fetch the case. I will see him out."

They passed the new maid in the upper hall, her dark eyes watching them with a touch of malice. Eliza lifted her chin in a motion much like her mother and continued to the attic without word.

Claudio quietly closed the door behind them for a moment of privacy. "I think the maid suspects us. Have you confided in her?"

"That nasty trollop? She'd be fired by now if it was up to me!" Eliza handed him her suitcase and spoke in a lower tone. "I'll see you tonight."

His free hand caressed her arm. "A nap would be good for you. You may dream of our wonderful life in New York." He touched her crucifix with a finger. "I love you."

She kissed him quickly on the lips and he took her right hand. Slipping off her glove, he lifted it to inspect her palm.

"What are you—"

"I thought you might have paint-stained hands and wore the gloves to hide them from your mother. This one is clean." He reached for her other.

"No!" She hid her left hand behind her back. "I'm sorry, Claudio, but my hands are clean. You should go before Mother comes looking for you."

"Until tonight at Jackson's Oak, *la mia Rose*."

"I'll be there, *amore mio*."

Eliza spent the rest of the afternoon in the attic drawing pictures of Sean. When she returned to the main floor two hours later, she found Leroy setting the table in the dining room.

"Please inform Mr. Campbell that I will be riding after supper but that I will see to Flora myself, both before and after."

"Yes, Miss Eliza."

"And please burn these in the stove." She handed him the sketches of Sean's likeness and joined her mother in the parlor until supper was announced.

When Rosemary carried the serving platter into the dining room, the cook frowned at Eliza. No doubt Leroy had shown her the drawings before he burned them. Rosemary had often told her how much she enjoyed Sean's visits. He had a way of sincerely complimenting the help and no one—besides her mother—could find fault in his disarming smile.

"Are you feeling well, Miss Eliza?"

"Yes, thank you, Rosemary."

"She looks much better having resting after the deacon left," Ruth said as she snapped open her linen napkin.

Eliza smiled at the cook. "The soup smells wonderful."

She would have preferred her final meal at Seacliff Cottage be more than the light fare her mother insisted on before the men arrived, but Eliza knew if she left through the kitchen on her way out, she could pilfer a roll or a few slices of bread for her ride.

Not until Rosemary placed the chilled grapefruit half in front of Eliza did she approach the topic of her night's activities with her mother. "I'm going for a quick ride after I finish eating."

"Nonsense, Eliza. It is much too late. In the summer you may take after-supper jaunts, but it is dark as pitch out there."

"The moon is full and the sky is clear. I'll just go down to the bay and back. No more than a mile."

"It is not safe."

"But I neglected Flora on my last visit, as I said earlier."

"After some ridiculous promise to Sean?"

"It wasn't ridiculous because it helped him feel better about me coming here alone."

"So you'll disobey your mother after following the wishes of that buffoon?"

Eliza stabbed the grapefruit with her serrated spoon and pushed back from the table. "Sean is not a buffoon!"

"You have done nothing but make a spectacle of yourself with that man since he first came here. He indulged you too much and now you shirk my rules, have gained too much weight, and I do not even want to think what he has coerced you into doing when I am not around. No good has come from this match!"

"The greatest blessing has come from my relationship with Sean because I now know how loathsome my parents truly are. I'd do anything to escape your and Father's tyranny!" Eliza ran for the hallway.

"You get back here this instance, Eliza Rose Melling!"

She fled up two flights of stairs, yanked her clothing off, and grabbed her forest green riding habit she had at the ready. Once her clothing and boots were on, she slung her black caplet around her shoulders and thundered down the stairs.

"Eliza!" Ruth shouted from the foot of the main stairs.

She ignored her mother and rushed down the back stairs into the kitchen. Rosemary looked at her from the sink and Leroy and little Priscilla stared from the table in the corner.

"I'm sorry for her upset, but I have to go." Eliza saw the concern in their dark eyes. "I appreciate you all. Goodbye."

Only when she laid the saddle pad on Flora in the stable did she remember she'd failed to grab some food. Hoping Claudio would think to secure a picnic for travel, Eliza placed the saddle on her horse. Flora whinnied and flicked her tail agitatedly.

"There's no time for that."

Eliza buckled everything on Flora, then her boot was in the stirrup and she mounted. Spurring Flora toward the lane, she fought to calm the snorting horse unused to winter night journeys.

On the ride to Daphne, Eliza's eyes filled with tears as she thought of all she'd left behind as the hooves trampled the dirt road. Her canvases, clothes, and comforts. And Sean—though she refused to leave all of him behind. Her grip on the rein tightened and her engagement ring glinted in the moonlight. She would always treasure the token of his love and the memories of their moments together.

Coming into town, the horse whinnied and reared. Eliza kept her seat and patted Flora's neck.

"Easy, girl."

The horse bucked sideways.

"Come on, Flora. Don't let Sean's dream from the other week spook you. We're almost to Claudio. You're always good when he's in the saddle."

***

Claudio buttoned the wool coat over his new white shirt in hopes of keeping out the night air. It was cooler than typical, and the absence of his cassock made him feel vulnerable. He walked to the forested area around Jackson's Oak and left their two suitcases in the bushes alongside the road. The full moon took the place of a lantern on his journey, like a message from God that he was on the correct path. It had to be right, for a life without Eliza was as horrific an idea as burning in purgatory.

Fifteen minutes early to the eight o'clock meeting, he took a moment to kneel in prayer. Clutching the priestly crucifix he refused to part with, he spoke aloud in supplication.

"Father, if it is Thy will to see me married to my heart's true love, send me a sign of Thy blessing. Our love seeks divine guidance. Help us on our path in life so Thy will can be done forevermore. Amen." Claudio stayed on his knees beyond the natural clearing the massive oak created by its shadowed girth.

In the distance, Flora whinnied with what sounded like panic. Her pace was erratic, not at all like her usual steady trot. Claudio stood as Eliza emerged from the south. The horse bucked into the clearing, moving sideways toward the tree. Eliza struggled to keep a firm hand as she shifted in the saddle, but the horse was clearly in some kind of distress. Had an animal startled her?

A moment later Flora reared, catching Eliza before she could reseat herself securely in the saddle. In a haunting motion that seemed too slow to be real, Eliza pitched off the horse head first. The sickening crack of her skull on one of the gnarled roots that clawed the soil echoed in Claudio's mind sevenfold. He lurched toward his fallen angel as Flora bolted in fright.

"Dear God, my Rose!"

Claudio pulled Eliza's still form onto his lap and rocked her in his arms, kissing her face and baptizing her in his tears. Then he saw it in a shaft of moonlight on her gloveless hand—Sean's engagement ring. Confused thoughts besieged his mind.

Why did she not return it in November?

Had she worn it to corroborate our story of eloping lovers because I did not have the funds to buy her a ring?

I could never afford such splendor as she is used to.

Why did God take her?

She never broke her engagement to Sean.

God has spoken and you are not worthy!

Claudio rose to his feet, carrying his beloved to the rectory so he could send word to Seacliff Cottage.

***

Two days later, Claudio alighted from a borrowed wagon along with Father Angelo at the Montrose cemetery.

"There he is," Ruth Melling said. "I must be comforted by Eliza's spiritual advisor. She loved her talks with you, Claudio."

Mrs. Melling made an imposing sight in her full mourning veil and black ensemble, but Claudio took her gloved hands and made kissing motions toward her shrouded cheeks. "*Signora* Melling, my heart aches for you and your family."

He turned to Alexander but was met with a harsh stare. Beside Alexander, Sean came forward to hug Claudio.

"Thank you for seeing to her as you did." Sean's voice hitched. "Carrying her through the night rather than leaving her to the whims of nature and then running for help is a kindness I can never repay."

"It was my honor," Claudio whispered.

Sean acted like a heartbroken fiancé, not a jilted former lover. The vision of the diamond ring on Eliza's hand burned in Claudio's mind, but he could not believe she had used him to escape her parents. Her love had been as true for him as his was for her. It had to be!

The family had not transported Eliza's body to Mobile for a graveyard burial because Ruth Melling wanted a mausoleum built for her daughter at Seacliff. The community cemetery would be her temporary resting place, though the thought of disturbing her humble sleep for a marble palace was nauseating to Claudio.

At the close of the service, Father Angelo spoke to Mr. and Mrs. Melling. Claudio went for the wagon, but Alexander caught his arm.

"I know this is your doing," he hissed.

Remorse filled Claudio's eyes with the weight of the blame. "I did not make Flora throw her."

"She was going to meet you." The icy gaze and set of his jaw made Alexander look exactly like his father.

Claudio lowered his head with shame, and Alexander walked away.

Sean watched the gravediggers fill the hole by the shovelful until Mr. Melling led him to the carriage in a rare act of sympathy, although it left Mrs. Melling alone.

"May I see you to the carriage?" Claudio asked her.

"Will you return with us, Deacon? I am alone in my grief."

Arm through hers, he walked slowly, unsure of her visibility through her veil and the tears he knew were in her eyes. "I cannot today, *Signora* Melling."

"You must visit me soon. I am staying at Seacliff until Eliza is laid to rest in her new home. Please take tea with me on Wednesdays."

"I will try to arrange that. But for now you have your husband, your son, and Sean."

"Never speak his name to me! It is *his* fault Eliza is dead. By his encouraging lead, she became reckless and dismissed my rules. She constantly fled to Seacliff unescorted, put on too much weight, and I fear he took liberties with her. They were much too free in their expressions of love." She clutched her handkerchief to her heart. "Once he leaves for Mobile, I never want to hear the name Sean Spunner in my home again. He ruined my daughter!"

Claudio nodded, though part of that guilt was his cross to bear rather than Sean's.

When they stopped beside the carriage, she raised a glove to his cheek. "Why cannot all men be like you, dear Claudio? I will see you Wednesday. Do not disappointment me."

He stared numbly after the Mellings' carriage until Father Angelo put a hand on his shoulder.

"Come, my son." He spoke in Italian. "I know you were close to the family. I will give you time each day to grieve, but service to others is the best healing balm. Remember that. This afternoon the Trione family could use help clearing their yard in preparation for a new vegetable garden. Will you go?"

Claudio nodded, eager to serve the Lord as penance for his sins. He would attempt to guide others to the path of happiness while steering them away from choices that led to overwhelming heartache—a road of possession and lust he knew all too well.

THE END

Bonus Short Story

"Dashing Through the Snow"

A Possession Chronicles short story

Sean Spunner sneaked through the kitchen while the cooks prepped dinner for his uncle's household. It wasn't a completely successful exit. Althea, the assistant cook, caught his eye and winked at him before he closed the back door.

Outside, he raised his face to the falling snow and opened his mouth to catch the snowflakes he hadn't seen for several years. Mobile rarely got snow, and today's weather with multiple inches accumulated had halted all normal activity in the city. Sean watched his breath puff out as the freezing temperature made his face ache.

In an attempt to stay warm, he ran down Palmetto Street, his feet making satisfying crunching sounds through the inches of snow. He didn't stop until he got to Washington Square Park. The gaslights around the square flickered against the ice and snow, giving a magical luster to the neighborhood park at twilight.

"Spunner!" John Woodslow shouted as he sprang out from behind a bench and ambushed his best friend with snowballs.

Laughing, Sean scooped up a handful of snow and hastily packed a ball to throw back at his friend. After several rounds—all with John victorious—they silently signaled a truce and came together.

"Did you do it?" Sean asked when they were a foot apart.

John grinned and tugged down his blue knit cap over his blond hair. "I sure did."

John was fourteen—ten months Sean's junior—but he was more experienced in the scheme of life. He'd told Sean that morning that he was going to deliver a Saint Valentine's Day card to the Easton twins and promised to meet Sean in the park to report about it before supper, no matter the weather.

"Did you give one to both of them or make them share?"

"Neither. I only left one for Cora. That way she'll know I'm serious about her and don't want her sister."

"So you signed your name?"

"You bet I did."

"But your signature is atrocious. She probably can't read it."

"Her loss." John shrugged.

"You did that on purpose because you know if a sixteen-year-old girl knew a boy your age gave her a Saint Valentine's Day card, she'd laugh in your face."

His fair complexion showed a hint of a blush in the dim light. "At least I was brave enough to leave a card, unlike you, Scholarly Spunner."

Sean had known John since he first came to his uncle's house as a twelve-year-old orphan. In an attempt to catch his nephew up to his new peers of the highest social class, Patrick Finnigan had pushed Sean academically, setting him up to become the top student within two years after transferring to the private school. Sean knew his uncle didn't want the other boys looking down on him as the poor orphan from the wrong side of town, so he supplemented his education during the school breaks and made sure he was in top physical shape to defend himself through a place on the school's boxing team.

"I couldn't have gotten away today even if I wanted to deliver a sappy card to some girl," Sean said. "Uncle Patrick had a list of reading for me to do as soon as he heard the school was closing due to the weather."

"We'll start out early tomorrow, before he can disrupt our plans," John said. "Meet me here at eight in the morning. There'll be snowball fights and maybe sledding if we can find something to use."

"I'll be here." Sean brushed the snowflakes off his hair and hurried home.

* * *

Sean threw his quilt to the floor, eager to greet another day off. The gift of no school on a Friday during Mardi Gras season was too wonderful not to take full advantage of it.

The fire in his bedroom hearth was almost out, but he wouldn't need it. Why spend a moment inside when there was at least half a foot of snow outside to enjoy? He snatched a pair of long underwear from his bureau and took yesterday's pants off his bed's footboard, not caring if they were rumpled. White shirt buttoned and tucked, he grabbed his socks before scurrying for the stairs.

"You better slow down," his cousin Megan called from her bedroom.

He skidded to a stop outside her room at the top of the stairs and leaned against the door frame as he pulled on his woolen socks, balancing first on one foot then the other. Megan sat at her dressing table, brushing her brunette locks. At fifteen, she wore her maturity like a badge of honor, draped in a bustled red dress befitting a morning at the cathedral rather than a stroll in the snow.

"Are you going outside in *that?*" Sean said.

She gave him an exasperated sigh. "It's better than dirty trousers and a smelly shirt. My mother wouldn't let you step a foot outside dressed like that. Be glad she's in bed with a head cold."

"I refuse to be joyful over Aunt Cecilia's poor health." Sean eyed Megan's ensemble when she stood. "I suppose you want to look like a cardinal, complete with a big tail rump."

"You're a buffoon, Sean Francis Spunner!"

"And you used to be fun."

He ran down the stairs, fleeing the memories of his childhood visits to this house and the capers he and Megan used to go on together—neighborhood frolics and household catastrophes. But all that had been before his parents died and Megan grew breasts. She had been kind to him that first year he'd moved in, and her friends had doted on him. But as the years passed they'd grown apart, boys against girls.

When Sean reached for the boots he'd left by the front door the evening before, Patrick Finnigan spoke from the dining room door. "No so fast, young man. There's something I need you to do today. Join me."

"But I told—"

"Now, Sean."

Still holding his boots, Sean gazed from where his uncle had disappeared into the dining room to the freedom beyond the frosted glass of the front doors. He sighed.

On her way to the kitchen, Althea paused on the pretense of checking the potted palm in the entry hall. Her dark face leaned close as she rubbed a frond between her thumb and finger.

"Breakfast, Sean Francis," she whispered. "It won't take long. Besides, you won't get far on an empty stomach. Cajun sausage and grits—a hearty meal to keep you warm all morning."

Sean dropped his boots and they both straightened. Nodding, he grinned at the woman in possession of the one voice that always gave him sound logic.

His uncle lifted his freckled face upon Sean's entrance into the dining room. Uncle Patrick's fine auburn hair was similar to his deceased sister's, making Sean—with his thick brown mop—appear to take after his father's family at first glance. But their tall, sturdy frames were similar.

With a nod, Uncle Patrick crossed himself. Sean followed his lead and sat reverently for his uncle's uttered prayer over the food. Althea stepped in from the kitchen as soon as the blessing was said and poured coffee for the man of the house.

"Sean, just because you aren't going to Spring Hill for school today," Uncle Patrick said, "doesn't mean you have a free pass."

Sean glanced up from ladling a big helping of grits into his bowl.

"I have an important delivery I need you to bring to Melling and Associates," Uncle Patrick said. "Then I expect you home at noon in time to wash up for midday dinner."

"Yes, sir. I can do that." Sean stabbed two large sausage links from the platter Althea held.

Uncle Patrick did the same when Althea came to his chair. "I know you can. And I expect you at your studies this afternoon."

"With all that snow outside, Uncle Patrick? This doesn't happen every day, or even every year."

"You're nearly fifteen, Sean. It's time to hang up some of your boyish games and focus more on your studies."

"Boyish games?" Sean laughed. "No man is ever too old to throw a snowball."

Uncle Patrick tried to keep a straight face, but the corner of his mouth quirked. "Perhaps not, but there's much to keep up with if you're going to graduate early."

"Yes, sir."

Sean sliced the spicy sausage and stirred the pieces into his grits so he could eat quicker. When he stood to leave the table, Uncle Patrick met his eye.

"The envelope addressed to Mr. Melling is on my desk. Remember, you're acting as a law clerk on my behalf. He expects it by ten o'clock."

"Yes, sir." Sean practically collided with Megan on her way into the dining room.

"You might ask your junior law clerk to put on clean clothes, Daddy," she said.

"He'll have a coat on and be covered in snow by the time he crosses Government Street," Uncle Patrick replied. "No one can stay fresh for long in these arctic temperatures, Megan. Not even you."

After fetching the letter then tying on his boots and buttoning up his wool coat, Sean poked his head back into the dining room to bid them farewell.

"A hat, Sean," Megan chided. "Just like a child, you have to be reminded of everything."

Uncle Patrick looked up from the newspaper. "And a scarf, young man."

With a frown and glance at the mantel clock that showed his morning wasting away, Sean reached for the banister to haul himself back to his room. He met one of the maids hurrying down, his cap and scarf in her hands.

"Althea said you'd need these, Sean Francis," she said.

"Dear Althea saves me again." He set the green hat on his head, pulling it low about his ears, then he wrapped the matching scarf twice around his neck and smiled at the maid. "Thank you."

A minute later, he was at the corner, reveling in the freezing temperatures and sparkle of the snow-covered houses and trees as he pulled his leather gloves from his pocket. It had snowed enough after nightfall to cover the prints from the previous day's pedestrians. The blanket of white crunched under his feet as he traveled another block toward the park.

John Woodslow, wrapped in a black coat and topped with his blue hat, was building a snowman at one corner of Washington Square and sent a snowball straight at Sean. It struck him in the middle of his gray coat. Laughing, Sean hastily gathered a handful of snow and hit John in the back.

"I can't believe you came unarmed again, Spunner!" John reached for two more snowballs hidden behind his snowman and let them fly, striking first Sean's arm and then his thigh.

The battle continued several minutes, with John heavily armed and sporting a good aim against Sean's quickly formed weapons and haphazard throws while he laughed. Children and adults from the houses circling the park joined in the fun and games.

When Sean spotted priggish Kate Stuart mincing her way through the snow in a bright purple cape, he motioned John to his side and nodded toward the newcomer. She was only thirteen but already thought she ruled the world, or at least all the young ladies at the cathedral. John immediately understood exactly what his friend had in mind. They both set to work packing the tightest snowballs yet, unbothered that they were bombarded by a dozen strikes in the process.

As graceful as a choreographed cotillion dance, they moved across the park to get behind Kate. Another girl saw what they were about to do and gasped. Using the girl's exclamation as a signal, the boys let their snowballs fly. John struck Kate squarely between the shoulder blades, jolting her forward. Sean's snowball struck just below her buttocks, marring the cape with a splattering of ice from its softer hit.

She turned with venomous eyes. "You rascals! I'll tell Father Quinn on you both!"

They laughed and escaped the neighborhood, not stopping until they reached Government Street. Clouds of air steamed before their faces as they caught their breath from the flight. The busy road typically teemed with streetcars, wagons, and carriages, not to mention pedestrians and horses, but now it was as clean and quiet as an empty field. Eerie, deserted, and calm.

Sean patted his coat where Mr. Melling's envelope was tucked into the interior breast pocket. Hearing the crinkle of paper, he relaxed to know he hadn't lost his special delivery. He checked his watch and was surprised that it was already heading for nine.

"I've got to go to Melling and Associates for my uncle this hour. Want to come with me?"

"Only if we can go through the district on the way. You can always see the finest horses in the stables behind the red-light houses."

Sean bit his lip and nodded. They had both grown up hearing about the tenderloin district, the area of town where some men went to be satisfied by women bolder than their sweethearts or wives—especially during Mardi Gras. The district had a mythical quality to boys their age, just a couple years shy of being old enough to enter one of the houses of ill repute located a handful of blocks northwest of the business section of town. Sean couldn't help wondering which of his friends would be the first to walk in as a boy and emerge a man?

He wasn't sure if he would, especially if he had fallen in love by then. After his parents died, Sean had promised God he'd be a faithful spouse like his father had been. He didn't want to be like his uncle and his society friends, who paraded their wives to masquerades and fundraisers only to indulge in sin at their own gatherings, especially during the weeks leading up to Lent.

Sean's father might have been a humble bricklayer, but he'd made sure his son was taught to be true to his religious and marriage vows, because he'd seen how—even as a young boy—Sean had been dazzled by the splendor of Patrick Finnigan's lifestyle, from the rich foods to the impressive personal libraries.

John led the way to Broad Street, instinctively staying on the unseen sidewalk like the other adventurers. At the intersection, Sean marveled at the vast expanse of snow covering all the streetcar tracks and horse dung typically seen in the road. Only a few marks marred the smooth snow, most likely left by the milkmen and newspaper boys.

With a whoop and a holler, Sean ran diagonally across the street. In the middle of the road, he dropped to his back and began moving his legs and arms to make a snow angel, laughing at the thought that it was probably the closest he'd ever get to Heaven. Especially with girls like Megan and Kate tattling on him all the time.

John was beside him a moment later, following Sean's lead. After leaving their divine mark, they ran north, snow and ice dropping off them like droplets from fog. Bells clanged and two racing buggies whizzed down Government Street, the young men at the reins oblivious to the pedestrians. The tracks made by the single horses and wooden boards instead of wheels sliced right through their snow angels.

"That's a bit of luck that we weren't still laid out on the road," John remarked, looking back.

"A blessing, not luck." Sean frowned at his marred angel a moment before heading north again.

Following the excited sounds of children and adults at play, Sean and John tromped through the fringes of the Creole neighborhood on their way to the red-light district. They paused to help a few girls build a wall for a snow fort and assisted a boy lifting a huge snowball on top of an even larger one to make a snowman.

"Stay and play with us!" the boy said.

"We can't," Sean replied, patting his coat. "I've got a delivery to make."

Another wagon-sleigh passed, spraying icy snow behind the rickety runners. The riders sang about jingle bells as they rode. Sean's nose was beginning to ache from the cold.

"This way." John motioned down an alley between Cedar and Lawrence Streets.

He led Sean toward a stable that serviced several of the brothels. The young man on duty was huddled in a pile of straw just inside the open doorway.

"Is it okay if we look at the horses?" John asked.

The fellow grunted. "Ain't many here today. Guess the gents are keeping their wives warm in this weather."

Sean knew John recognized most of the thoroughbreds in the city and knew who owned them. His father took him to the riding club a couple times each week, and he was on a polo team with several other young men from the parish. Sean enjoyed riding every once in a while, but he preferred boxing. For now, the break from the chilly north wind was appreciated, though it pained his nose more as the feeling returned to his face. There were three horses in residence but only one captured John's attention, a chestnut stallion in the furthest stall.

"It's Janus!" John reached out a hand to stroke its muzzle.

"Don't go touching 'em," the stable hand called out.

"But I know this one."

"No touching unless you want to pay to keep me quiet. And you'd have to tip me better than the fancy man who rode him in. I doubt you can afford that." The stable hand tucked his dark hands under his armpits. "What, is it your daddy's or something? You out spying for the old lady?"

"Nothing like that," John said. "This horse belongs to my friend Al—"

"No names given here!" the stable hand remarked. "But I doubt the gentleman would appreciate being called a friend by a mere boy like you."

"He must have taken his son's horse because Janus is younger and more spry than his own." John defiantly stroked the horse and then rushed out through the rear door.

Sean stumbled after him as the shouts from the worker chased them from the stable. In their hurry to escape, they went further north, out of their way. At Lawrence Street, they doubled back south and encountered a mixed group of bawdy women playing in the snow. They didn't look like much, all bundled in ill-fitting coats with their hair in disarray from the wind.

"You boys lost?" a brunette called out.

"No, ma'am," Sean replied, trying not to gawk at her chest that peeked from beneath her fastened cape.

"Y'all best move on then," she said. "You're not old enough to be paying visits here."

"Maybe they're wanting work," a blonde said. "You boys want to shovel snow from a few walks for a nickel?"

John laughed. "How about for a kiss instead?"

The brunette shook her head. "Don't sell yourself short, young man. You'll have girls lined up to kiss you, if they're not already. You don't need her used lips."

Sean checked his watch and elbowed his friend. "I have to deliver that envelope. Are you staying here or coming with me?"

"You'll be a charmer too," the brunette said to Sean. "But if you want to pay me a visit in another year or two, ask for Hazel. I've turned many boys into men in this city."

"Thank you, ma'am." Sean gave her an uncomfortable smile.

"Do I know your father?"

"He's dead." Sean refrained from insulting her by saying that his father never would have come to this neighborhood. "I've got to make a delivery now. Enjoy the snow, Miss Hazel."

Sean walked away without waiting for John, but he heard his footsteps crunching after him.

"Goodbye, ladies!" John called before reaching Sean, then he said, "That's Alexander Melling's horse in there. He got Janus for his birthday last autumn. Mr. Melling must have ridden him this morning and might be in one of these houses with a woman. You should have asked those ladies if they knew him.”

Sean shook his head. “Like the stable hand said, these people don’t deal in names. At least not without a price.” He increased his pace. “Besides, I doubt my uncle would appreciate me delivering one of his correspondences to a red-light house. I was instructed to bring it to Melling and Associates by ten o’clock, and I will.”

They hurried on without conversation, turning left on St. Francis Street toward town. Sean ignored the snowballs hurled at them, though John did pause to lob one back if they were struck.

“Should we stop in the cathedral to confess to Father Quinn before Kate gets to him?” John asked when they approached Claiborne Street.

“Maybe on the way home.” Sean looked at his watch and stepped up the pace more until he slid on a patch of ice.

“You better slow down,” John said. “I’m not going to carry you if you twist an ankle.”

Sean started a shoving match that ended when they were both on their backs in the snowy road. Laughing at each other, they stood and Sean threw an arm around his friend.

“Hold it together a couple more blocks, Woodslow.”

When they reached the north side of Bienville Square, Sean gazed across the road to the trees frosted with snow, like the fancy cakes his aunt served at tea parties. Icicles hung from the three tiers of the fountain, winking in the morning sun like sequins on a Mardi Gras mask.

Sean gripped the slick brass of the doorknob at Melling and Associates, difficult to do with his gloves on. It finally turned and he stepped into the space he had visited many times before, both with his uncle and as a runner between offices. No secretary sat at the front desk, nor did he hear any clerks in the file room. John followed him inside, closing the door behind them.

“Hello?” Sean called from the bottom of the stairs. “I have an important delivery for Mr. Melling!”

The man himself came down the stairs, smoothing his cravat. He paused a few feet in front of Sean, his blue eyes staring coolly as he took a drag on a cigarette.

After whipping the cap off his head, Sean ran a hand over his unruly hair. “Good morning, Mr. Melling. I’m here with a delivery from Solicitor Finnigan. Six inches of snow can't stop the legal profession from rolling forth."

Mr. Melling laughed. "You're Patrick's nephew, aren't you?"

"Yes, sir." Sean shoved his cap under his arm and opened his coat to retrieve the envelope.

"I remember you from last summer. Bright mind, good worker, quick on your feet, and a sense of humor." He exhaled a cloud of smoke. "How old are you?"

"Fifteen in less than two weeks, Mr. Melling." Sean handed over the envelope.

Melling tapped it against the wall. "Do you have your eye on law school?"

"Yes, sir. My uncle already has me studying for it alongside my classes at Spring Hill."

"Excellent. There's nothing like a young man who applies himself." He paused to puff on his cigarette, his eyes flickering to John standing near the door. "Is that you, Woodslow?"

"Yes, sir." John took a few steps closer, taking the cap off his blond head.

"Did your father get you a new stallion for Christmas?"

"Yes, sir. He said it wasn't right for a boy as young as Alex to have a better horse than me on the polo field."

Mr. Melling laughed, eyes brightening. "Nothing like envy to spur a man along. Janus is an exceptional horse. I rode him into the city today since my carriage couldn't make it. I refuse to allow the coachman to remove the wheels for a rare day or two of snow."

"Are there proper facilities nearby for a horse?" John asked with a lift of his fair brows. "The community stables don't offer enough protection in this weather."

Mr. Melling cleared his throat. "I'm using a private stable, not too far from here. Janus will be well seen to."

"That's good to hear, sir. Alex loves that horse."

"Now, young man," Mr. Melling said as he turned to Sean. "How would you like to be a junior clerk at Mobile's most prestigious law firm this summer?"

"Thank you, Mr. Melling, but Uncle Patrick has my schedule planned out for the next five years."

"He's putting you to work for his gain, no doubt. Do you need to stay for a reply?"

"Not that he mentioned, sir, but we'll be in the square for a few minutes if you need to call me over."

"Very well. Regards to your uncle, and to your father, Woodslow."

The boys hurried out the front door, pausing on the sidewalk to don their caps before dashing across the street, where they crafted a few snowballs. John elbowed Sean and motioned to an approaching sled-buggy.

"It's the Eastons. Well, almost half of them."

"The good half," Sean said with a smirk when he saw the three oldest sisters riding with their older brother, Maxwell.

Cora and Emma were close friends with Megan, and Sean could never keep his eyes off the Easton twins when they visited at the house. Halos of blonde hair, blue-grey eyes, and perfect curves on their still-budding bodies were enough to make any boy ogle them. And with their oldest sister Susan looking like a full woman at seventeen, the odds of the fifteen-year-old twins being perfection in another few years were good.

"Let's ambush them," John said.

"That's not the way to get the attention of girls like those."

The sled whooshed past them, the twins in the back waving.

"I'm not waiting around to quote poetry to them." Expecting Maxwell to circle the park, John took off across the square to cut them off on the other side.

Not wanting to be left behind, Sean ran after him. The Eastons slowed for the turns, and Maxwell flicked the reins to increase their speed once they were on Dauphin Street. Staying several feet away from John so he wouldn't be mistaken as the ambusher, Sean watched with open mouth as his friend's true aim clocked Maxwell on the shoulder. The snowball burst, showering Susan with the powdery ice.

Maxwell immediately pulled the horse to a stop, and by the time he'd thrown the reins to his sister and jumped out of the sled, John was running. But Maxwell was bigger and faster. He tackled John in a snowdrift at the base of a lamppost.

"You might have hit one of my sisters, Woodslow!" Maxwell yanked him around, but instead of pummeling John's face, he punched him in the stomach several times then ground handfuls of snow into his mouth.

"Aren't you going to help your friend?" Cora asked Sean as he stood beside their buggy.

Sean shook his head and stepped onto the runner, peering at the twins, warm within their lap blanket and furs. "I told him not to do it. He deserves the beating."

Emma giggled. "You could have stopped him if you wanted."

"I was too overcome by the beauty within this sleigh to intercept him." Sean grinned and started reciting a Keats poem. "'O thou whose face hath felt the Winter's wind, Whose eye has seen the snow-clouds hung in mist—'"

"Enough of that, Sean," Susan snapped. "You're too young for any of us here. Try your poetry on Lucy in a few years. She'd appreciate it, at the very least."

"She's the bookworm, not us," Emma said.

"Susan is too." Cora straightened her shawl. "But as she said, you're too young for us."

"But you're sweet and adorable," Emma said. "Never change, no matter what Megan says." She leaned over and kissed him on the cheek.

To Sean's despair, his face was too numb to tell how soft her lips were.

"Emma, you minx!" Maxwell left John lying in the snow and stomped over. "Don't make me beat up two boys today."

Emma lifted a shoulder in a coquettish way. "Sean meant no harm. He was only reciting some Victorian drivel about winter snow."

"Spunner, go!" Maxwell pointed toward John. "Make sure Woodslow gets home without trouble. I tried not to rough him up too much."

"How about giving us a ride?"

"It's the least you can do, Max," Susan said. "He's just a boy having fun. You didn't have to jump on him like that. He's still holding his middle."

A cloud of breath escaped Maxwell when he sighed. "Get in, the both of you, before I change my mind."

Sean went to where John was sitting in the snow and hauled him to his feet. He pushed him toward the front bench, next to Susan who had shifted closer to her brother.

"I'm sorry I struck you with the snowball," John told Maxwell as he took a seat beside Susan.

"Sorry you did it, or sorry I caught you?" Maxwell asked.

"Both," John admitted with a grin.

Sean climbed in the back row, snuggling between the twins when Emma pulled the lap blanket aside with a naughty smile. He knew he'd enjoy every minute of this ride.

"Maxwell, would you be able to go around the square once more?" Sean asked. "I see Mr. Melling leaving his office, and I need to make sure he doesn't have a message for my uncle."

"So now I take directions from my younger sisters and from random boys as well?" Maxwell muttered.

Susan poked her brother in the ribs, and Maxwell steered the horse around the corner. Mr. Melling, turning to the sound of someone calling his name from next door, slipped and fell on his side. Several men and ladies rushed over, including a newspaper reporter.

"Could we be of assistance?" Maxwell asked when they reached the scene.

"Do you need to get to the hospital, Mr. Melling?" One man pointed to Maxwell. "These folks have a sleigh."

"It's just my elbow—nothing to fret about." Mr. Melling was clearly trying to downplay his embarrassment. "I'm not as old and decrepit as that, gentlemen and ladies."

Sean stood, knocking the blanket to the floorboard. "Any message for Mr. Finnigan, Mr. Melling?"

"No, thank you. I'll be in touch with him next week." Mr. Melling held his arm and tried to disperse the audience.

With nothing to be done on their part, Cora tugged Sean back to the bench and Maxwell set the horse back to a trot. The twins lowered the lap blanket simultaneously, trapping Sean's arms beneath. As they flew over the snow-covered streets of downtown, Emma's hand found his, their gloved fingers intertwining. She brought his hand to her knee and pressed it against her leg. Sean bit his lower lip.

Maxwell half-turned to check on his sisters. "Spunner, you get your hands above that blanket right now or I'll beat your—"

"Max!" Susan shoved him as Sean brought his hands straight up, over his head. "You're barbaric today. You can put your arms down, Sean."

John shot his friend a sneer of pure jealousy as Sean settled his arms around each of the twins' shoulders. Emma and Cora giggled, causing John to turn back with an annoyed huff.

Emma's hand—still beneath the blanket—went to Sean's knee. As though not wanting to be outdone, Cora set her gloved hand on his opposite thigh. Sean nearly melted into the upholstery at the stimulating weight of their hands on him. He could sit forever between such heavenly beauties, but he wished he could return the attention.

Before he realized it, they were turning down Broad Street and onto Palmetto, stopping before his uncle's house. Megan, still in her ridiculous dress, was building a snowman in the front yard. Seeing Sean tucked between her friends, her pleasant face fell into shadow.

Sean quickly kissed Emma's cheek and then Cora's. He nimbly hopped over Emma's leg and landed on his boots in the dirty snow on the well-traveled sidewalk.

"What do you think you're doing, Sean?" Megan asked with annoyance.

"Telling my seat-mates farewell." He spun back to face the buggy and pulled off his cap to bow. "My thanks, Easton family. It was most enjoyable."

"You don't have to be nice to him," Megan said as she approached her friends.

Emma giggled when Sean winked at her. "He's charming."

"He's wearing yesterday's dirty clothes!"

"Who looks at clothing when a fellow has a smile like Sean's?"

Sean bit his lip at Emma's flattery. Megan frowned at the twins.

"Max clobbered John," Cora said.

"I did not!" Maxwell's knuckles strained against his black gloves.

"He isn't handling the cold well," Susan said. "And we wanted to make sure the boys made it back in one piece."

"The only thing I'm not handling well is being outnumbered by sisters!"

"There were three females and three males in this sleigh for the last few minutes," Emma pointed out.

"Lucky me," Maxwell grumbled. "Next time I'll bring along Edmund, Peter, and Aaron so we don't need to pick up stragglers."

"No," Emma whined. "Big brothers are the only type of brothers to keep around."

"They're the only useful ones," Cora agreed.

"Let's go home, ladies," Maxwell said and then smiled at Megan. "The snow agrees with you, Miss Finnigan. I'll turn the care of these ruffians over to you. Hopefully, you can keep your cousin and his friend out of trouble.”

John crossed his arms. “We don’t need watching.”

“I would disagree,” Maxwell said as he signaled the horse to move.

Emma waved at Sean as they pulled away. Relishing the attention, he was oblivious to all else, so Megan’s shove sent him to the ground.

“Hey!” He jumped to his feet, not bothering to knock the snow from his backside.

John inched away, laughing over Sean’s predicament. “I’ll see you later!”

Ignoring John’s retreat, Sean turned to his cousin. “What did you do that for?”

“Keep away from my friends, Sean Francis!”

“I can’t help it if they wanted to share their lap blanket with me.” He gave her an arrogant smirk.

“You filthy jackanapes!”

Megan lunged at him, but he was ready. Rather than shove her and possibly ruin her red dress or crush her bustle, he clasped her arms to her side and loomed over her with his superior attitude.

“I won today, Megan. Accept the fact that even in wrinkled trousers, your younger cousin attracts more females than you attract men in your fine gown. Although Maxwell Easton did pay you a compliment.”

“I’ll have you know I’ve had dozens of kind words from people as they walked by this hour.” Her chin lifted and she looked away, unable to move as Sean still held her.

“Is that why you’re building a snowman in that dress—to attract men? That’s pathetic.”

“You don’t know anything!”

“But I do. I may still be young, but I can tell you that men don’t want a woman they’re afraid to touch. If you want interaction more than fleeting comments, go change into something a boy wouldn’t be afraid to strike with a snowball.”

“Don’t be ridiculous! And I don’t want the attention of boys anyway.”

“Sure you do. Boys come in all ages.” Sean released her arms, flipped her velvet cape, and nodded toward the house. “Go change into a regular dress and coat. I bet you a nickel you'll have a flirtation within ten minutes of returning."

"From a boy my age or older?"

"Sure enough, but plenty of younger ones too, I'll wager. You're pretty, Megan. Don't let high fashion stand in the way of possible beaus."

She pursed her lips and marched into the house. Sean set to work building an arsenal, piling the balls behind Megan's snowman so they wouldn't readily be seen from the road.

"Sean Francis!" Althea called from the porch. "I've got a cup of hot cocoa if you want it."

He left his work and wiped his gloved hands on his trousers as he climbed the steps. "Thank you, Miss Althea."

"If your nose gets any redder, it's going to fall off. Wrap that scarf around your face after you're done drinking."

He took a sip of the hot sweetness. "It's not bothering me."

"Because you can't feel it. That's not good, child." Her hands were on her slim hips, mouth set in a straight line.

"Thank you for caring about me, Miss Althea, but I think I'll survive until dinner."

"You better. I've got your favorite bread baking, and a hearty stew for y'all."

"That sounds wonderful, but what about you standing out here with no coat?"

"It'll help me work faster to warm up when I go inside."

Sean knew she was waiting for his cup, so he drank the rest as quickly as he could without burning his mouth.

"Thank you, Miss Althea. It was delicious. I feel warmer already."

Megan joined them on the porch. "You need to quit coddling him, Miss Althea. He's got a high enough opinion of himself as it is."

"And for good reason, Miss Megan. Sean Francis is the best boy that ever roamed these halls."

Megan rolled her eyes as Althea went back into the house. Sean took in the length of Megan's black skirt, made full from functional petticoats that would keep her warm, and the gray wool cape that hung over her plain blouse.

"Don't you feel better?"

"I suppose I do." Megan straightened the cuffs of her lined gloves.

"I've set you up with a supply of snowballs here," Sean told her as they stepped into the yard. "Don't be afraid to use them."

"What do I do? Stand around and wait?"

"Play, build, frolic." Sean motioned to the snowman. "Make that bigger for a start. Do you want me to help?"

Megan nodded and set to work making another tier while Sean padded the base with more bulk.

Freddy Davenport, a lively twelve-year-old who was best friends with Edmund Easton, came whistling by.

"Nice snowman, Sean," he said.

"It's Megan's. I'm just helping finish it."

"You did well, Miss Megan," he said with a blush, too well-mannered to say more.

"Thank you, Freddy." She'd seen him enough times at the twins' house to know him by name, though he didn't attend the parish.

"There's going to be a battle at Eddie's house at two o'clock," Freddy added.

"I'll be studying, but thanks," Sean said. "Be sure to tell John. He might be at the park."

Freddy nodded and stuck his hands in his coat pockets, continuing on his way.

"Little Freddy doesn't count," Megan said before Sean could breathe an *I told you so*.

He was still laughing when a group of boys a year or two older than him strolled by. They stopped, elbowed each other in a way that meant *look at her*. One boy let a snowball loose, striking Sean on the side of the head, and another got Megan on the chest.

"Sorry about that!" another boy said as he crossed into the yard. "My friends are a bit rowdy today. Are you all right?"

She nodded.

"I'm Mason," he said as his friends on the sidewalk threw snowballs at him.

Megan laughed as she brushed the ice off her cape. "I'm Megan, but please don't stand too close if your friends are going to keep throwing those."

Sean discreetly pointed Megan and her visitor to the pile of snowballs tucked away. They glanced at the cache and then at each other with a nod. In one swoop, they gathered armfuls and started tossing them at the boys on the sidewalk. Grinning, Sean took a seat on the front steps and watched his cousin behave as she hadn't in years.

Megan and Mason rallied their efforts as they fought two against four. When they ran out of pre-made snowballs, she ripped apart her snowman to toss chunks of it at the boys, laughing the whole time. The battle ended with her sitting on the frozen ground and Mason shielding her.

"That brother of yours ain't worth much!" one of the boys shouted. "He sat it out and watched you get walloped!"

"He's my cousin, and he had a rough morning!" Megan called back.

Surprised at Megan's defense of him, Sean watched as Mason helped her up and invited her to visit the soda fountain he worked at for a complimentary drink.

"Could I bring Sean with me?" She motioned to him still on the steps. "He's the one who stocked the snowballs."

"Of course, but come sometime after the snow clears. I don't want you risking yourself on account of a measly soda."

"Thank you, Mason." She gave him her best smile—the genuine one. "I'll see you soon."

When he got back to his friends, they jostled him and looked back at Megan several times before making it to the corner. She waved the first time and then pretended not to notice. But as soon as they were out of view, she plopped down beside Sean, resting her head on his shoulder.

"Thank you."

"For what? According to them, I sat around like a lump."

"I'm glad you did. The battle wouldn't have been as magical if you'd participated."

"It wouldn't have been much of a fight if I hadn't stocked the ammo for you either. Not to mention, it never would have happened if you were still wearing that cardinal showpiece."

She sat up straight and scooched away a few inches. "That's doubly true. You helped in every way and made this the best day of the year so far. What can I do to repay your thoughtfulness?"

"The only thing I'd like is to be on good terms with you once more."

"Then don't be annoying. Cease chasing my friends, and—"

"I'm never going to be perfect, and we're bound to see the worst in each other from time to time, but if you could show me some respect like you—"

"You're no longer a mournful boy."

"I'm still an orphan." He let his lower lip pout and gazed at her dolefully.

"That doesn't work on me, Sean Francis." She shoved his shoulder. "But I'll try to be nice, so long as you keep away from my friends."

"Then I'll admire them from afar."

"Not if you know what's good for you."

"Empty threats, dear cousin."

Megan grabbed a handful of snow and shoved it in his face. "That wasn't empty, was it?"

She jumped up and ran, and Sean chased her down Palmetto Street.

"Don't forget you owe me a nickel!"

She laughed and slowed until he caught up with her.

Sean raised his brow. "Do you want to join the neighborhood fun like you used to?"

Megan nodded and they united for the snowball battle in Washington Square.

John got clobbered.

THE END

Author's Note

Many thanks to the readers who voiced questions about the year between *Perilous Confessions* and *Murmurs of Evil*, wanting to know what exactly happened with Eliza Melling because they enjoyed her in the first book. I knew what happened but not all the details. It was an adventure revisiting the characters after completing all eight novels in the series and discovering that Eliza had even more scandalous secrets than I imagined—especially Sean Spunner. (Dalby's Darklings members know how I feel about him.)

If you are new to The Possession Chronicles, I hope you enjoyed visiting and will return for more. With each instalment of the series, I dig deeper into the history of the Mobile Bay area so I can present the most accurate story possible. That being said, I do sometimes take liberties but the notable changes can be found in the acknowledgement sections of the different books or in special blog posts on my website. If you ever have questions about fact verses fiction in the world of The Possession Chronicles, I'm happy to answer questions via email or social media connections. Thank you for reading.

And a special note of thanks to Joyce Scarbrough for her stellar editing and my family for their support.

About the Author

While experiencing the typical adventures of growing up, Carrie Dalby called several places in California home, but she's lived on the Alabama Gulf Coast since 1996. Serving two terms as president of Mobile Writers' Guild and five years as the Mobile area Local Liaison for the Society of Children's Book Writers and Illustrators are two of the writing-related volunteer positions she's held. When Carrie isn't reading, writing, browsing bookstores/libraries, or homeschooling her children, she can often be found knitting or attending concerts.

Carrie writes for both teens and adults. *Fortitude* is listed as a Best History Book for Kids by Grateful American Foundation. She has also published *Corroded*, a contemporary teen novel about friendship and autism, several short stories that can be found in different anthologies, as well as a multitude of Southern Gothic novels for adults.

For more information, visit Carrie Dalby's website:

carriedalby.com